Vigilante Justice

David Jarvis

ISBN: 979-8-218-94388-2

Contents

Chapter 1

"You have cancer, Dave".

That's how Dr. Langston, my doctor of fifteen years, broke it to me. As simple as that. I sat in the exam chair that exists seemingly in all these small, clinic-consulting rooms. Situated around me were the typical accouterments of such a room. Beside me on my right sat the blood pressure machine. On the other side sat the keyboard into which Dr. Langston typed his notes. Across the room a small counter with a sink and faucet took up a small portion of the room. Underneath the sink were cupboards where cotton balls, towels, and various objects resided that helped the good doctor and his aids care for the patients examined in this room. I looked at him, not wanting to believe what he told me, yet somehow excited by the news. *At last. This is almost over.*

"How bad is it?" I asked. He looked back down at his clipboard before answering, and I knew the answer was bad.

"Well," he began, "It's Stage 4. With the options we have today; new therapies, medicines, we can prolong life for quite a while." *Did I really want that? Longer agony?*

"I assume operating won't work, eh?" I asked flippantly. He looked at me for a minute.

"No," the doctor said. "It's too far into your system; too deep. If I operated, there wouldn't be much left of you when we were done."

"Humph!" I muttered, "That's encouraging." I paused, waiting for him to say something else. When he didn't, I swallowed hard and asked him the sixty-four-dollar question.

"How long, then?" I wasn't sure I wanted to hear the answer, but that's what they always ask in the TV shows and movies, isn't it? *How long until I'm dead?* The doctor straightened up a bit, looked me in the eye from about four feet. A deep, intense, hangdog, intensely sad look.

"Well, it's hard to say. Eighteen months, couple years at the most. You might go into remission. Who knows? But normally, the pain will grow as you progress. Your appetite will decline, you'll feel sick more and more often, get weaker and weaker, until finally you won't want to get out of bed."

"Hell, who wants that? Doesn't sound like much fun to me," I said. He motioned for me to get dressed. I got out of the chair and started pulling on khaki docker slacks, a blue polo shirt, and my black Rockport shoes. Nobody ever said I was a fashion model. The doctor seemed embarrassed watching me dress and busied himself with updating my file on the computer. He pulled a small prescription pad from his lab coat pocket and wrote something, tore it off and handed it to me. "I've given you a prescription for when the pain starts. You'll need it. Otherwise, there's little more I can do." He walked toward the door and opened it. Turning in the doorway, he looked at me with deep sympathy in his eyes.

"I'm really sorry, Dave. I wish I had better news," he said. He shook my hand, turned, and walked out into the hallway, closing the door behind him.

Chapter 2

I finished dressing and paid my bill at the front desk. After receiving my after-visit summary, which outlined what we had discussed in the room and further advice on handling symptoms, I walked out of the clinic. There seemed little to say about life at this point. My wife Grace passed away from cancer a few years ago, and my two kids were grown and departed from the house where they grew up. We kept in touch but got together infrequently. The kids were involved in their own lives now, leaving little time for me. I didn't begrudge them that. I did the same with my parents when I was their age. Anyway, the life I had left was not much of a life to cling to, in my opinion.

I walked to my Ram 1500 Tradesman parked nearby at the curb. Using the electronic key fob, I unlocked the driver's side and got in. The cool feel of soft fabric felt nice against my back as I started the engine. Looking both ways a couple times to make sure the road was clear, I pulled out into traffic and away from the clinic. I thought about what I should do with the time remaining to me.

I wasn't retired, at least not completely. After we stopped working, Grace and I became park hosts for the Oregon Parks and Recreation system for a few years before she died. We enjoyed it so much I kept on after she was gone. In exchange for a few hours of work cleaning yurts, cabins, tent campsites, and running a few odd errands, we received free space for our trailer, an eighteen- foot Rockwood. We liked to do our stint near the beach, as we both loved the ocean. After Grace passed away, I continued to work the parks, moving from park to park per the state rules. I continued because the ocean was like an old friend, and the waves soothed my soul. They had aided me through some dark times, like when Grace was sick, slowly fading away from me. She lay there dying on the hospital bed, and there was nothing I could do. The waves gave me whatever peace I could extract from a world I wasn't sure I believed in anymore. Work the state parks gave me was easy, and only occupied a few hours a day for a few days of the week. The rest of the time was mine, which I spent walking the trails, gazing out over the waves, watching the boats come and go, and people playing on the beach. Gray whales journeyed the Oregon and Washington coasts from March to May and again from December to January. I made it a point to watch them as often as I could. I was always going to be a successful best-selling author, but never quite accomplished it while Grace was alive. Now, nothing held me back, but the passion was hard to capture after lying dormant for so many years. A pastor I once listened to said God gives talents to every person for him or her to use in this life. However, if they don't use them, he gives them to someone else. Don't know if I believed that, but I struggled to pull the words out with just the right inflection to say just the right thing in just the right way. I hoped it would come back to me in time.

Overall, my life was good, I guess. Except, the whole reason for living wasn't with me anymore. I was hanging on, waiting for God to decide my time was up and take me home without too much pain. The last thing I wanted was a lengthy, drawn out illness that devoured my insides. Suicide had occurred to me a few times, even before my latest diagnosis or before Grace got sick, but something always stopped me. I kept thinking I could always do it when things got bad, but they had yet to get so bad that I couldn't take one more day. Now this. My time was up. I was dying. Unfortunately, it appeared that God hadn't listened to my prayers and granted me an exit both painful and mundane. A quiet whisper of a life, gradually fading until no longer there at all, was not to be mine.

I pulled onto Highway 101 and headed back down to my trailer at Bullard's Beach State Park, located south below Coos Bay, Oregon. One complication of living in the state parks is that you could only do it for a few weeks at a time, sometimes longer than that, but never over ten weeks. At the end of that time, you moved on to another campground, then another, and so on and so on. I had a regular route throughout the summer, but I also maintained a small house in McMinnville, where I usually spent the winter, and I would move there soon this fall when the colder temperatures would be upon me. I lacked the desire to be a snowbird, honestly. Occasionally, I enjoyed hunkering down in familiar settings.

As far as the cancer was concerned, I was going to get a second opinion, of course. My doctor was a good friend, and I liked him a lot, but he was, alas, a small town doctor living in Coos Bay, half retired himself. As quickly as I could, I would investigate a more state-of-the-art facility when I was near a big city, likely Portland. But in my gut, I felt he was right. I hadn't felt very good for quite a while.

After pulling into my campsite, I locked the truck, then unlocked and stepped into the trailer. The trailer wasn't a huge monster. Grace and I just wanted enough room to feel comfortable in it without feeling as if we were driving our house around the countryside. The trailer had a couple pull outs, so once we settled in our campsite and weren't moving around, it seemed quite spacious. The kitchen was small and neat, the way I liked it, and the living room contained a couch, a couple of easy chairs, a recliner facing the television, and the dinner table. Toward the back was the bathroom, complete with a toilet and shower. In addition, some closet space was in the bedroom. Grace had added colorful curtains to the windows, which added more charm. Comfortable, but not shabby. My contribution to the trailer was a large Samsung HD TV hung on a wall in the main living space. With a satellite connection, I got terrific reception for the TV and amazing speed for my computer. After using the bathroom, I turned on the TV. Television these days was crap, in my opinion, but some wonderful shows existed. I didn't watch the news too much, especially when I was eating because it depressed me. However, tonight I switched it on while I made myself steak, onions, and rice, one of my favorite meals.

Bullard's Beach State Park is close to Bandon, Oregon, about a hundred miles north of the California border. The beach was spectacular, giving the best of both worlds. Walking beaches where the waves caressed the sand. A thin arm of a jetty stretched out into the ocean, and the waves crashed against it in stunning beauty. Fantastic rock formations jutted out of the sand just on the other side of the Coquille River, where the ocean displayed its awesome power, hurtling itself against the rocks. A very rewarding place. Not too crowded either, most of the time. Bandon's beach overlook loop offered visitors the opportunity to explore on foot or view from their vehicles.

I often made my way 30 miles north to visit Shore Acres, a state park that offered another incredible view of the ocean. Grace and I were married there many years ago. Pictures of the wedding and other beach events hung displayed on the walls. Sometimes I would get them out with some videos we had and look at them, remembering all the times Grace and I had shared. She was my life for so long; it was hard to exist without her.

Atop an 80 foot bluff, overlooking Bullards Beach, stood Sunset Oceanfront Lodging. We stayed there often before we were married, and then off and on through the years. Not a fancy place, but it had a magnificent view of the ocean, which is why we chose it. Even after we purchased our trailer, we still parked in the truck at a lookout point near the motel and gazed out at the waves.

Tonight, while steak sizzled in the frying pan and I cut up onions to throw in, I flipped to find a national channel and settled on one I could tolerate. At least it appealed to my somewhat limited interests, and I half watched it while frying the steak, making rice, a side salad and sipping on a glass of ice water. Soon everything was ready, and I sat down to eat at the kitchen table. I'd barely eaten anything for lunch and was eager for this meal.

The news was filled with the same old shit that made me stop watching in the first place. Unrest in the Middle East leading to a minor fracas over something or other; North Korea had launched another rocket, despite all the sanctions. A robbery here, a car accident there; it went on for a while and finally wrapped up with a promise to provide more news about everything tomorrow night. Blah, blah, blah. I turned down the volume and began cleaning up the dinner dishes, tuning things out and thinking about switching channels when the local news started. An attractive female talking head began the news with a voice over some video playing in the background. I was in the kitchen and washing dishes, so I didn't catch all the storyline, which sounded interesting. By the time I retrieved the remote, the station had announced other news items it would cover over the next hour. "Well, that's just great," I muttered to myself. "I find something interesting and now I have to wait for it."

Assuming it would take a few minutes for the news station to come back around to the story, I went back to finishing up the kitchen. Often the station baits you with a top story, and then uses it to keep you hooked until the last few minutes of the show before they run it, which infuriated me. I would give them a chance to run the story at the outset. If they didn't, I'd switch to another channel or turn the TV off altogether. Aargh! But they pissed me off! After the dishes were clean and the kitchen put in order, I settled down in my recliner and got comfortable. Following the dinner meal, I liked to stretch out in my chair and relax a bit.

As I suspected, they didn't run the story again until the second half of the program. Typical bullshit. So inevitably, the one story I was interested in only got a sixty-second summary. The reporter began speaking with a video playing softly behind them showing a large crowd of angry people. It suddenly switched to a young man exiting the local correctional facility.

> "***In tonight's news, protestors gathered outside the courthouse to protest the release of convicted child sex offender Raymond Justman. Justman was released today after serving a three-year sentence for the sexual assault of an eleven-year-old boy. Many people say justice was not served, as the boy, Tommy Morgan, still has nightmares from his ordeal, and continues therapy.***" The scene switched from the reporter to the angry red face of Tommy's father. "***That bastard stole my boy's innocence and ruined him for life! Why's he getting out now after only three years? Why isn't he dead or put away forever? My son will never be the same because of what this monster did to him. He can't sleep, He can't—***" the camera shifted back to the reporter again.

> ***"Neighbors in the area wonder where Raymond is going to live, now that he is free. He will first need to register as a sex offender wherever he goes. The community, needless to say, is not happy with this development. Janice Compton, KYXZ News."***

And the news moved on to the next story.

"*What a sad ordeal for that young boy,*" I thought. "*And to think it only got a sixty-second blurb.*"

Damn! How much pain and suffering did that boy endure? And now his tormentor is out to begin again. This country is really beginning to suck. I thought about my wife and where she had worked as a counselor in a center for molested and abused children. She told me several particularly nasty stories about some children she worked with. Over time, I came to feel a general disgust for a substantial portion of the human race because of what I learned about these monsters and what they did to kids of almost any age. Rape, sodomy, torture, dismemberment, and more. Sometimes these bastards got caught, and then Joe Public learned how depraved these losers could get. Some taped their madness for later replay. Others felt disgust at what they'd done but continued to do it. Why, I couldn't fathom. It lay beyond my imagination.

I watched the rest of the news until eleven, then considered watching a movie but decided against it. I just wasn't in the mood. I picked up my paperback sitting on the little table next to my recliner, and settled down to the remainder of my evening with a book. The book told the story of a serial killer on the loose in Los Angeles. The police seemed unable to find clues, but the detective assigned to the case was playing out a hunch about who he thought the killer was. Although the book was good, I was tired from the stress of the day. Slowly my head drooped, and the paperback slipped from my fingers to the floor. Gradually, I became more relaxed and drifted into sleep.

Chapter 3

I began dreaming about a young girl running from a man through a dark forest. She looked to be about eleven, with long, dark hair and a simple dress. She wore white socks with sneakers. I seemed to be running with her and was terrified, just like her. Behind us, the man closed in and he grabbed the girl and flung her to the ground. He fell on top of her and began tearing her clothes off. She lay under him screaming and I kneeled beside her head, watching her face, unable to help. She abruptly ceased screaming, swiveled her head to me, and stared at me with large, soulful eyes. While the man brutally assaulted her, she spoke to me.

"You could have stopped him, but you didn't try. Why didn't you try?" Then she just closed her eyes and went limp.

My eyes jerked open, and I lurched up in the recliner, instantly awake with the adrenaline shock you get after a vivid dream. My book lay on the floor. I scooped it up to place it on the table by the chair. Standing up, I shook myself to relieve the shudders and stepped into the kitchen for something to drink. Jesus. That dream shook me. It was so real. I remembered virtually everything, especially the man attacking that young girl and her words to me, which penetrated to my soul.

"You could have stopped him, but you didn't try. Why didn't you try?"

Chapter 4

The next day was dismal, with clouds and a drizzling rain. Typical Oregon weather. I saw it was a mess outside, so I stayed in the trailer playing a video game and surfing the internet. The news story from the night before haunted me, along with the dream. After my character in the game died a few times and I sat there exasperated, I elected to do some research on child molesters. At my browser's input page, I typed "child molesters" and got over ten million hits on the subject. "Well, shit, that's a lot of hits," I said out loud. It didn't really bother me, though. The most relevant items would sort toward the top. I dove in.

Many of the first entries were sex offender registries that listed all registered offenders in my area. Names, photos, addresses, and crimes showed across several websites. Further down were articles about analyzing why child molesters do what they do. I picked one and brought the article up. The article was filled with a lot of unnecessary information like "defining the purpose" and "making accommodations." I scrolled down to get to the main point.

"Hmm," I said to myself. "This looks interesting." The article began talking about the general statistics regarding child molestations. It was interesting all right, but it showed how sick our society really is. Most molesters are people known to the victim. Mostly men, but sometimes women, too. Most activities take place at 3pm, just after school lets out, or between six and eight pm. Most predators made it a point to get into positions allowing them access to young children, as a counselor or a coach, or a babysitter. As I read, it became clear that not all perpetrators were monsters hiding in the bushes, waiting to snatch an unsuspecting child. No, it was worse. Much worse. Most times, it was a person the child trusted the most.

I thought about this and the television news report from last night. The report talked about concerns raised by neighborhoods and where Justman was going to live. It didn't talk about the eleven-year-old boy or his relationship to Justman. Was Justman any relationship to the boy? Maybe Raymond was an uncle or a cousin. Perhaps he was a counselor. I wasn't sure I cared enough to find out. Hearing about it was heartbreaking, yet I had my own issues. I stopped looking at the report because I was more concerned about rehabilitation and repeat offenders. News reports discussed the inaccuracy of the sex offender registry, and the numbers were not good. As of 2020, over 747,000 registered sex offenders are in the United States alone, according to one source. However, that was just the documented and registered ones. And it didn't differentiate what kind of offenders they were, or if they were likely to repeat their offenses. And what about those that skipped? What about the clever ones not discovered yet? And, even if registered, did that keep them away from children? As I stared at the monitor I knew I didn't know the answer to that, but I resolved to find out.

I tried another tactic and logged on to a sex offender registry. This one didn't ask my name, so I didn't have to fill out a profile or anything. I punched in my zip code and seven offenders popped up within the city of Coos Bay, with a history of their offenses, where they lived, and a photo.

"Well, that was nice of you to do that," I said to myself. "Let's check some of these addresses out." The time was nearly two-thirty pm, about the time school let out. I wasn't busy doing anything and looked up the location of at least one of these bastards. The GPS system on board the computer displayed the addresses, and I printed them out before I put on my jacket. I got in my truck and drove to the first residence on the list.

Michael Bateman lived in a small, older two-story house with a gabled front porch, painted willow green with a white trim. I parked a few houses down and shut off the car, with the front of the car facing the house. According to the website, Bateman was thirty-five years old, five foot ten, and weighed one hundred forty-five pounds. His convictions included four counts of sodomy and attempted rape of a minor child. That was the extent of the information available on the web. However, I knew if he were still at it, he would reveal himself in his activities. I wondered how long I could sit here and not draw attention to myself. Maybe longer than I thought, as most of the homes around Bateman's house appeared to be vacation rentals, and appeared empty.

My research back at the trailer revealed three elementary schools in the area less than three miles from Bateman's residence. One of them was less than a mile. I could not believe the courts would allow this, and I was certain the neighbors wouldn't if they knew who he was and what he did. Maybe there was a reason Bateman lived within a bunch of rentals. Fewer people around to snoop on him. I sat in my car for about an hour when Bateman drove up in an older white Toyota Camry. He parked in the driveway and went into the house without looking my way. *Good,* I said to myself. *Very good. He doesn't know I'm here.* I could see him through the windows, moving about the house, but I wasn't too sure of all his activities. He came back out and got in his car. As he pulled out and headed north on Herman road, I followed him at a discreet distance. He drove to the parking lot of Cherry Grove Elementary school and parked in the teachers' section. I pulled in and parked a few car slots over where I could watch and saw him enter the building through an employee entrance. I couldn't help wondering what Bateman was up to.

Grace told me once that standard terms of probation for child predators were no contact allowed with minors or they could not be within three hundred yards of any facility that housed children. So, what the hell was Bateman doing here? And how could I find out? I thought of one or two ways I could get in to the school. However, if I went up to the office and asked for Michael and they went and got him, I'd be in a fix. I could say I was new in the area and wanted to start my child in school here. But I certainly didn't look the part of a parent with a younger child, now did I? And if I managed to get past the office, what would I do then?

This entire line of speculation gave me pause for thought. What was I trying to get myself into? Bateman had clearly violated his parole.

The least I could do was turn him in, rather than any direct action to Michael Bateman himself. By reporting him, they would take him off the streets. Or so I assumed. I started the truck, pulled out of the parking lot, heading up the street away from Bateman's house. If I called the police, I wasn't going to get any more involved than just letting them know about Bateman's parole violation. I didn't want to use my cell phone or my landline. Therefore, I needed a pay phone. That proved to be a small problem.

The cell phone craze nearly wiped out the demand for pay telephones practically overnight. The phone companies began pulling them out or not bothering to repair them a few years after cell phone sales took off. It took me a while to find a pay phone that worked. I finally spotted one next to an older grocery store and pulled into the parking lot. Getting out, I walked to the phone and lifted the receiver. Before dialing, I looked up the Sheriff's department. Placing fifty cents into the slot, I dialed the number. It rang twice before someone picked it up.

"Sheriff's department, can I help you?" The voice was female.

"Uh, hello," I started blandly. I hadn't thought this through. I wasn't sure what to say.

"Yes, can I help you?" asked the receptionist again in a no nonsense voice.

"Uh, I want to report a sex offender in violation of his probation, but I don't know who to contact," I said.

"I'll connect you with the Special Victims Unit. Your name, please?"

"I'd rather not say," I said.

"That's fine. I'll put you through." It was as easy as that. A minute passed. Then I heard sounds of a phone being picked up.

"Hello? This is Lieutenant Anderson, Special Victims Department."

"Ah, Lieutenant. I want to report a child predator in violation of his probation. His name is Michael Bateman."

"Excuse me, who is this?" Anderson sounded impatient.

His abrupt manner helped get my nerve back. "I'd rather not say. I just wanted you to know that Michael Bateman, a convicted child molester, is currently working at the Cherry Grove Elementary school."

"How do you know that?" asked Anderson.

"You don't need to know how I know. You simply have to go pick him up. All I'm doing is trying to be a responsible citizen and remove this creep from our streets."

"OK. Here, let me write this down. You say the person's name is Michael Bateman? And the school is Cherry Grove Elementary?" I could hear this Lieutenant Anderson writing on what I presumed was paper.

"That's right," I said.

"Hmm. Interesting. Well, thank you, we'll check it out." And the line went dead.

"You're welcome, prick," I said to a dead receiver. That didn't go quite as I expected. I thought they would stumble over themselves in gratitude that a citizen helped to capture a sleazebag. Oh well, at least I turned him in. I started the truck and pulled out of the parking lot and headed home, certain I had helped to clear the streets of scum like Michael Bateman. On the way, I went back to the school and wait for the police to show up and nab Bateman. I wanted to be there when he was arrested.

The school parking lot had emptied some, now that the school day had ended. I pulled into the lot but parked in a different spot than before, where I could still see the main entrance. I expected the police to arrive in several cars and charge through the main entrance, handcuffs out, moving in to arrest this reject from humanity. To avoid being spotted, I hunkered down in the truck so the police wouldn't see me and proceeded to wait. And wait. Then I waited some more. After two hours, no police showed up. The main doors of the school opened and Bateman walked out, heading, to his car. *No, no, no, this isn't how it's supposed to happen*! *Where are the police?* I wanted to jump out, grab Bateman, and shout to the school, "Here he is! Here's the child rapist! He's not supposed to be here!" But I didn't. I just watched in awe as he drove away. *Maybe the cops are busy right now and they'll grab him at home,* I thought to myself. *Yeah, that must be it. I'll go watch his house.*

I started my truck and flew down the street toward Bateman's residence. His car was already in the driveway and I parked in the same place as before. Again, I sat myself down to wait. Again, I waited. And waited. And waited some more. What was going on? I was getting sleepy. It was nearly eight-thirty in the evening and the strain of the day, coupled with my lack of food, left me feeling nauseous. Finally, at nine o'clock I said to hell with it. If they were going to get him tonight, it would be without me. Maybe I'd read about it in the morning. I started my truck and drove to my trailer. Tossing my keys on the kitchen counter, I made myself a tuna sandwich, grabbed some veggies from the 'fridge and sat down to watch the news. The local news made no mention of any arrest of a predator in violation of their parole. I was a little put out the police hadn't responded faster, but I figured my job was done. I had turned in a child rapist.

Once again, the events of the day caught up with me and I fell asleep in my recliner. And again, the dream came to me. It was the same dream, and it filled me with as much dread as before. Once more, I was jogging alongside the girl. As before, the man, I couldn't see his face, caught up to her and roughly threw her to the ground. Again, he assaulted her while I lay frozen next to her, watching her face and hearing her scream. Again, she turned to look right into my face. And again, I had to listen to her accusations, her breath truncated after each word as his heavy thrusts knocked the wind out of her. "You could have stopped him, but you didn't. Why didn't you try? Why didn't you even try?"

CHAPTER 5

The next morning was Thursday. Still overcast from the day before, but it had stopped raining. After watching the news on the TV while eating breakfast, I decided to move on to the next predator on my list. I would check on Bateman later. Pulling up my notes, I discovered that my next target, Justin Fox, lived over on the North side in a much nicer neighborhood than Bateman. It would be harder to blend in, as a Ram truck often isn't the vehicle of choice in these areas. SUVs and fancy cars were more the norm. Observing Fox while in my truck would prove challenging. After I got there, I watched for about half an hour. But when an elderly woman with a small rat looking dog walked by on the sidewalk and looked at me with a frown on her face, I knew I should leave.

Hmmm, this one is going to be harder, I mused. Too many people about. How do I check up on this guy? I decided to come back after dark. To occupy my time, I used my GPS to locate the other seven predator addresses. Once I reached each location, I surveyed the area, jotting down notes about where and how the house or apartment complex was situated on the property. I noted what cameras I could see and what lighting might be like once night fell. Around one o'clock I found myself near one of my lunch hangouts, so I ducked inside and joined a few of my fishing buddies often found there. After ordering a beer and a nice, fresh halibut fish sandwich with fries, I joined my friends. One of them, sitting next to me, was a surfcaster, roaming around the beaches and fishing where he saw fit. He looked every bit the beach bum, wearing flip-flops, shorts and a patterned t-shirt. His long, brownish hair usually flipped here and there around his face when he was outside and in the wind. The weather was turning, so he also wore a light windbreaker while he sat at the table with the guys. He turned to look at me.

"Whatcha' been up to, David?" he asked. I pondered for a moment what I could tell him, decided nothing about my recent activities was information I cared to share, so I simply smiled.

"Not too much," I said. "Just watching the ships go in, then watch 'em go away again. How 'bout you?"

"Caught some nice perch the other day off of Bullard's beach," he replied. "They were a lot of fun," he said. "Tasted pretty good, too." I smiled at him.

"That's good," I said. "You might even start to break even, eating what you catch with how much you spend on bait. What do you think?" We both laughed.

"I don't know. I use quite a lot of bait, I can sure tell you that. Maybe I should just eat the bait, like in sushi." All the guys smiled at that. "Yeah, that might make better sense," I replied, chuckling.

After lunch, I left the guys still talking about imagined catches and drove to stake out the Cherry Grove Elementary school and see if the police had picked Bateman up yet. It dismayed me to see they had not, as I recognized him going into the school when I pulled into the parking lot. "Well, shit," I said. "What the hell is going on? Why haven't the police picked him up yet?" I got angry. I pulled out of the school parking lot and raced out to the same phone I had used before and dialed the police station.

"Hello, I'd like to speak to Lieutenant Anderson please," I said in my politest voice.

"I'm sorry," said the receptionist. "Lieutenant Anderson isn't in right now. Can I put you through to his voicemail?"

I hesitated to say yes, as though my conscience was warning me about something. "No, that's fine. Do you know when he will be in?"

"I really couldn't say, sir. Is there anything else?"

"No, I'll call back later." I hung up, enraged. *What the fuck was happening around here?*

I knew it wasn't terribly bright to call from the same phone, but I couldn't believe the police hadn't arrested Bateman yet. I was getting more and more upset the more I thought about it. The circumstances brought to mind the stereotype the police just didn't care. Well, dammit, I cared. It wasn't anything complicated. Though I wasn't abused or anything, and nobody else in my family had ever been abused, I still possessed the ability to care about the well-being of little children, didn't I? Christ, did someone have to be abused to care what happened to the youngsters in this world? Shouldn't regular, decent people care about getting these monsters off the street? I know I did. And I was going to do something about it, one way or another.

Chapter 6

Lieutenant Anderson stopped by the receptionist on his way back to his desk. "Any messages, Mavis?" Mavis broke her gaze away from the computer monitor and looked at him over the rim of her glasses. Anderson thought she was quite attractive, and easily the smartest person in the department. Why she worked for him for the last ten years eluded him, but he was sincerely grateful for her presence.

"No messages, Lieutenant, but someone did call, asking for you."

"Who was it?" he asked gruffly.

"Well, that's just it. He didn't give his name or want to be put through to your voice mail. It sort of sounded like the man who called yesterday."

"Okay, thanks."

As he sauntered back to his desk, Anderson reviewed the calls he had received and deduced that the caller may have been the one for Michael Bateman. Several burglaries and a couple of murders had kept him from responding to this unknown caller's information sooner. Before he forgot about it, he decided to check this Michael Bateman out. He punched up the name and received a response almost immediately. Four convictions of sodomy with a minor, one attempted rape. That was just the start. This guy was a genuine piece of work. Now, where did that guy say Bateman worked? Something Elementary School. Something starting with a C. A soft ch- sound. Cherry? Cherry Elementary? That sounds about right. Anderson brought up Bateman's' data that included the license plate of his car. His telephone rang, and that was as far as Anderson got.

Chapter 7

While waiting for night to fall, I packed myself a snack of a ham sandwich. Made with mayonnaise, horseradish and some pickles. I included chips and water to round out the repast, and drove out to my favorite spot overlooking the beach. Leaning back against a rock, sheltered from the wind, and witnessing the waves crashing against the rocks was exhilarating. No two waves were the same. Each had a unique pattern rolling toward the beach to expend its power on the rocks. Occasionally, two waves hit the same place on the rocks and crested magnificently in a shower of spray. I loved it here where I could hear the ocean, feel the wind against my face, and smell the salt in the sea air. This was where I came to do my thinking. No one disturbed me here. It was my quiet place. As I relaxed, I pulled out my sandwich from the small cooler I packed earlier and ate, admiring a flock of pelicans. Six in all, they soared in and out between the waves on some quest I could never figure out. They never dived for fish or some other morsel just below the ocean's surface. They always just flew about. I loved watching them, and never tired of the spectacle.

But life was changing. I needed to face that. I was sick and going to get sicker. My prescriptions would help me but the end would inevitably be the same. Eighteen months, the doctor had said. Two years at the outside. I hoped it would be longer than that. I'd heard many stories of people living much longer than their prognosis. Not a painful longer than that, but just a longer spell of life on this planet. When the time came for me to end, I fully intended to put a bullet in my brain. I did not intend to spend my last days in a nursing home. Lying in my own shit while listening to the yells of others in my room or down the corridor suffering from pain or dementia. No thanks. I'd much rather eat a bullet.

My thoughts turned to my activities over the last few days. What was I trying to accomplish? My time at Bullards Beach was ending and I would need to move on to the next site where I would set up my next park assignment. After that, it would be time to head for my home in McMinnville to wait out Old Man Winter. I wanted to see Michael Bateman pulled off the streets and put back in jail before I left for my next site. However, the police had yet to act, which totally frustrated me. One of the many things Grace and I discussed for hours was our combined exasperation regarding Oregon and the United States. We watched the news often enough to hear about the murders, robberies, and rapes that occurred throughout the country daily. But what we talked about most of all were crimes against children.

For me, it began with Westley Allan Dodd, who took delight in molesting young children, some as young as two years old. Reports said he molested near fifty children in his career as a serial psychopath. He raped, and then stabbed, two brothers, one who died in the woods. The other brother died in route to the hospital. The prosecutors asked for the death penalty, and the jury agreed. Westley himself asked to be hanged, as that was the way he killed his last victim. At his execution, the press was present to watch and provided testimony as to the humaneness of the execution. The courts executed Dodd in the manner of his request. Afterwards, each reporter recounted their eyewitness account of the event. Most described the twitching body, or how the corpse hung from the rope, as though we were supposed to feel sorry for this monster more so than his victims. But not one of them had the guts to say, "I'm glad the fucking bastard is dead." Which is what I would have said if I'd been there. Other monsters, like Ward Weaver, disposed of his victims in fifty-five gallon drums and buried them under his patio. These bastards were bad enough, but the molesters were the ones that really got to me. How could you possibly have sexual thoughts about a child four years old? Or even an eight or ten-year-old? It was just sick. Countless times I told Grace if I ever came across somebody molesting some kid, I'd pop them on the spot and save the state the cost of a trial. I have a concealed carry permit and usually went armed. Some things, I said, were worth going to jail for.

So, where was I going from here? Time was short. Let's cut to the chase, I told myself. *Did I aspire to be a hero? Go out in a blaze of glory, having swept the land clear of the scourge of child predators, making all things right in the world? Did I seriously think I could accomplish this?*

The answer was no, of course. I knew if I started doing what my heart told me was right in the big picture, nothing would change. The world would still hold its monsters; men who were evil would still walk the earth.

But what of the children I could save? What about the few lives I could spare the agony of these abominable acts? After all the talks Grace and I shared, could I honestly turn my back on these children, expecting a broken justice system to bring to accountability those who would commit these evil deeds? There would be no glory in what I was thinking, certainly no thank you from the legal justice system. If they catch me, the state could sentence me to life in prison or even execute me. Society would denounce me as a vigilante, taking justice into my own hands. And it would be true. Moreover, it might also be true that my journey would speak to others who would rise up against injustice and more people would stand together to protect our precious children.

Well, I said to myself. *Looks like I've decided what I want to do. If the justice system won't fix this, then I will attempt to. No glory, just the satisfaction that I did something to change the world and make it a more positive place.* I finished my lunch, watching the waves. It was a very satisfying day.

Chapter 8

Michael Bateman could feel the pull of his next victim, the want in his system. Working with the children at Cherry Elementary made him very much aware of what he wanted. All these delightful children running about, teasing him. Taunting him. He fought to maintain control, when all he desperately wanted to do was snatch one of them and haul them to his secret place. The place where he had fun.

He had been careless before and got caught, and they found his hideaway. The courts put him in jail, and during the day, doctors talked to him, and sometimes gave him medicine. But at night, his cell door occasionally opened. Men, both guards and inmates, would take him to their special place down in the basement. There they gave him a taste of his own medicine. He genuinely enjoyed it. It reminded him of his childhood, when father and his friends came into his room when Mother was away. They sometimes beat him; they always raped him. So, with this happening at night, did they actually expect him to be rehabilitated? If anything, he was worse when he got out than when he came in.

Ahh, but now he was free. He was registered as a sex offender, but that hadn't stopped the school from hiring him. This out of the way school hadn't bothered with an extensive background check, which was the reason he had chosen the school. He jumped parole in another state and began working at the school. Now he was set to make an abduction, maybe two, before he moved on. Just another couple of things to do and he would be ready.

CHAPTER 9

Lieutenant Anderson sank into his office chair, picking up his ringing phone as he fell into the chair. "Hello. Lieutenant Anderson. Yep. Yes, that's right. Yep. Okay, Right. Good job." He hung up the phone and leaned back. After a minute of speculation on another case, he browsed his desk and saw the memo he wrote to himself about Michael Bateman before he left the office earlier that day. He logged into his computer, accessing police records. Soon he had Bateman's record on his screen again. And the terms of his probation showed no contact with children and to register as a sex offender.

"Well Bateman, you stupid ass, if that phone call was correct, looks like you're going back to jail," Anderson thumbed an intercom switch. "Hey Stromberg," he called. "Get in here, will you?"

"Be right there." Jack Stromberg was a uniformed police officer who patrolled the area containing Bateman's last known address. A well-built man, physically fit, he liked to work out. Jack appeared in the doorway. "What's up?"

"We received an anonymous phone call that a Michael Bateman is in violation of his probation. I need you to find this character and figure out what he's been up to. He's a convicted child molester, and this call says he's working at the Cherry Elementary school over on Glendale, probably under an assumed name. Check on it and if he's there, bring the bastard in."

Stromberg was leaning against the doorjamb, but at the mention of a child molester he stood up straighter. Jack Stromberg didn't like child molesters. There was a better than even chance Bateman might have an accident with his face before he got back to headquarters.

"Sure, be glad to." He took the paperwork from the Lieutenant, going over the material. He hitched up his holster and sauntered out the door and into the hallway, picking up his partner as he went. Anderson turned back to his desk and started tackling the remaining piles on his desk. "One down, many more to go," he said to himself.

Chapter 10

The sun was low in the sky when I got back to the trailer. It was getting dark, and I ought to have been hungry, but I wasn't, truthfully. The temperature was dropping, and I wanted to watch the news to find out if the police had apprehended Bateman.

Tonight, the news focused on the economy and what a person could do to save money and make wiser investments. Boring stuff, actually. Still, it was good to pay attention to this sort of thing. Never know when you might actually learn something. I grabbed water out of the refrigerator, more out of habit than anything else, and sat down to watch the news. As the news progressed, it seemed they had not caught up with Bateman yet. Or, if they had, it wasn't public knowledge. Damn those bastards! Why didn't they pick Bateman up? I was getting more frustrated by the minute. If they didn't pick him up soon, I might take matters into my own hands.

The news ended, and I switched to a movie channel. During the show, my mind kept wandering to Michael Bateman. I had a bad feeling something was about to happen. Right after the movie ended, I went to bed.

CHAPTER 11

Finally, the day came. Bateman, in his capacity as the janitor, determined three boys who were perfect for his plans. As the days progressed after his employment, he watched his special children. Soon, their patterns of behavior revealed themselves. He needed to get one of them alone so he could overcome them and take them to his secret place.

The abandoned warehouse out away from town on Ripley Road. Away from prying eyes and sensitive ears. He focused predominately on Jordan Knightly. Jordan was ten years old, a shy little boy. He was friendly enough with the other boys, engaging in outside play as much as any of the others. He laughed and smiled often. But Jordan had a little secret.

Between the school and where Jordan lived was a city park. The park was sizeable, boasting many trees, picnic tables, plus trails for jogging and hiking snaking through the forest. Although it was possible to traverse the park and forest to reach Jordan's home, Jordan's mother adamantly forbade him from doing so. His mother was never specific about the why, just that "something bad" could happen to him on the way to or from school. Initially, Jordan obeyed his mother, and walked around the park, sometimes with his friends, to get to his house. Eventually, though, the boys started sneaking through the park after they determined no schoolteacher or parent was watching them depart the school grounds. The first few times Jordan was terrified, either from the "something bad might happen" scare or being caught by a concerned school employee or parent and ratted out to his parents. But after a while, nothing happened on either front and the boys took the path through the park all too often.

Only when they couldn't sneak away unobserved did they follow the rules and go around. Because through the park was a shortcut and took less time to get to their houses, the boys took to hanging out together for a short time to even out the travel time. That way, the parents wouldn't get suspicious. Jordan felt safe, traveling with his friends through this forbidden zone. Often they met hikers and joggers on the paths. So it felt pretty safe.

Today, however, was different. It turned out that Jordan's friends all had other things to do, so Jordan ended up going through the park alone. He didn't see anybody else on the path. And was getting nervous when he saw Mr. Bateman on the path ahead of him, picking up some trash and depositing it in a nearby trash barrel. It looked a little strange, but Jordan thought Mr. Bateman was helping to keep the park clean, just like he did at the school. He didn't know of any other janitor that did that.

Approaching the janitor, Jordan noticed Mr. Bateman seemed oblivious to his presence, and jumped when Jordan called out his name.

"Wow, Jordan! You gave me a start. Heading home from school, then? Where are your friends?" asked Bateman. Jordan looked around and behind himself, as though noticing he was alone for the first time. Mr. Bateman smiled. "It's OK, Jordan. I can see you're by yourself. You're getting to be a big boy, aren't you? You don't need the other boys." Bateman leaned a little closer to Jordan. He whispered from a little distance, "I know your mom doesn't want you walking through the woods without an adult, does she?" Jordan lowered his head, shaking it back and forth. Bateman continued his charade. "Your secret is safe with me. I won't tell anybody." Bateman started walking toward his car, which Jordan finally noticed parked just off the street and at the foot of a path leading into the woods.

"You thirsty?" Bateman asked. Jordan was actually a little thirsty. "Come on over here, then. I've got some apple juice I keep in a cooler in the car." By now, Jason was a little worried, but not too much. The whole situation seemed bizarre, not just the fact that Mr. Bateman and his car were in the woods. It wasn't until Bateman opened the door and stepped back from the car, saying "Help yourself," that Jordan could see there wasn't any cooler. He backed off, but Mr. Bateman grabbed him and threw him into the passenger side of the front seat. Jordan's alarms resounded urgently, but the opportunity had already slipped away.

He took in a breath to yell for help, but Mr. Bateman slugged him in the stomach so hard it knocked the breath out of him and he collapsed on the seat, gasping for air. Bateman dashed around the side of the car and jumped in. Jordan realized then the car had been running all this time. The engine was so muted he hadn't noticed. He finally got his breath and tried to scream again as the car began pulling out from the woods onto the street, but Michael smacked him across the face. "Shut up!" he hissed. Jordan tried the passenger side door, but it wouldn't open. Michael had fixed the door a few years ago to prevent any escape.

They sped to the abandoned warehouse Michael found a few weeks before. He dragged Jordan to the warehouse office where earlier he had placed a mattress, some rope, and a cooler. Michael stripped him, and then tied him face down on the bed, covering Jordan's mouth with duct tape. After removing his own clothing, he climbed onto the bed, trembling with excitement. It had been so long.

Over the next several hours, Michael assaulted the young boy repeatedly. Jordan screamed, but the duct tape over his mouth kept anyone from hearing. Besides, they were out away from other buildings, and it was unlikely anyone would have heard him anyway.

Early the next day, it was time for Bateman to get ready for work. He needed to go home first and clean himself up, so Michael satisfied himself one more time, then strangled the boy with a lamp cord he brought along for just that purpose. Placing Jordan's body in his car, he drove into town, stopping behind a store he knew had no cameras. There, he dumped Jordan's body in the store dumpster, threw some trash over it, and headed home. After his shower, Michael felt refreshed and ready to begin the new day. He drove on to Cherry Elementary without a care in the world. Life was glorious.

Chapter 12

I awoke the next morning with no particular agenda for the day. A couple of yurts needed cleaning later, but that wouldn't happen until after the tenants left. With checkout time at one pm, it would be a while before the assigned camp sites would be ready for cleaning. Just cereal and coffee didn't appeal to me this morning, so after my shower I made bacon, scrambled eggs, toast, with coffee. After making all this, I settled at the dining table. Finding the remote, I turned the TV on. The local news was rather startling.

> ***"Today's top story is the disappearance of ten-year-old Jordan Knightly. Last seen walking home, it's assumed, through Madison Park, which is next to Cherry Elementary School in Bandon, Oregon. Jordan was wearing a red shirt, blue jeans, and a light gray jacket. Police have issued an Amber alert. If you see Jordan, please contact the police at XXX-217-3671. In other news today–"***

I sat at the breakfast table, stunned, breakfast forgotten. A child taken! From Cherry Elementary! Could it possibly be true? Was Michael the cause? How could I find out? Several of my questions were answered after the next commercial break.

> ***"Police have taken into custody, Michael Bateman, in connection with the disappearance of Jordan Knightly."***

The television showed Bateman being placed in a patrol car, his head down and away from the cameras.

> ***"Michael Bateman is a convicted sex offender found working at the Cherry Elementary school under an assumed name and questions are being raised how that could happen. Speculation points to a lack of funds for a sufficiently deep background check at this school. Back to you, Nancy."***

I couldn't believe what I was hearing. A little boy taken virtually right next to the school. It sounded impossible, but obviously, it was true. And Bateman, taken into custody. Was it too late? I wanted to call the police station, but wasn't sure how smart that was. Someone could recognize my voice or recognize the phone number. That would end my crusade before it began. It made sense to make the call, but from a different phone. I got up from the table, and then it hit me. I was thinking like an old, retired person. Other methods of communication were available to me. I knew about cell phones and emails. Hell, I used a cell phone every day. But you could buy prepaid cell phones that gave you a phone number when you activated them. By using these phones and jumping around the carriers, I stood a far better chance of evading triangulation of my carrier signal.

I drove out of town as far as I thought feasible, then went to several stores that sold prepaid phones. They weren't that expensive, and I didn't buy ones with lots of time on them since I intended to use them once and then throw them away. Once this was accomplished, I found a place to park and got out, dialing Lieutenant Anderson.

"Anderson here."

I launched right in, unable to control my anger. "Why didn't you pick up Bateman when I brought him to your attention, you stupid shit! You had two days' notice of where he was working and you fucking did nothing! Because of you, a child is probably dead. Do you realize that?" There was a brief silence on the other end.

"Who are you?" Anderson asked. "What is your name and what business do you have with these circumstances?"

"My name is unimportant. I am a concerned citizen trying to help you do your job, but you aren't even listening to me."

"That's not true, mister whoever you are. If you had been more forthcoming with your name and your involvement in this affair, we might have acted sooner and picked him up. What are you afraid of?"

"I don't believe you. If you had talked to me face to face, we'd still be talking while you checked me out and that little boy would still be gone. Don't transfer your guilt to me. If this boy is dead, his blood is on your hands, not mine. Fuck you." I hung up, so frustrated and angry I was shaking. Fuck! Fuck! FUCK! This was not what I had expected from the police force. Not at all. I turned the phone off and threw it on the ground, grinding it beneath my heel. Starting the car, I drove around town until I settled down. I surprised myself by getting so incredibly angry. But a young boy was probably dead or dying and the police acted too slow to stop the man responsible. I was sure it was Bateman. Too many clues pointed to him.

CHAPTER 13

Lt. Anderson stared at the phone receiver for a second and then hung it up. He thumbed the intercom switch on his desk. "Mavis, I've got a nut who keeps calling me regarding Michael Bateman. I'd like to set up a trace next time he calls. Can do? He's probably calling from a cell or a payphone, but that's not a problem, is it?"

"Not really, sir, as long as he's not using a burner phone. That's what the dealers do. If he does that and keeps moving around, it will be impossible to triangulate him by pinging off the cell towers." Anderson contemplated that for a second.

"Well, let's wait until he calls and see if we can't figure out who he is."

"Right, sir. I'll set it up."

Chapter 14

Bateman was on all the news outlets the next day, held on suspicion of kidnapping. The day after his arraignment, Bateman made bail and surprised me by getting released. But then I read on the net that if an accused can satisfy certain criteria and post bail, the police can't hold them. Which was exactly what Bateman did. How he raised bail and convinced the judge he wasn't a threat to society or a flight risk baffled me. All I knew was that Jordan was still missing.

He hadn't come home yet and his parents were frantic. Standing before the press, Jordan's mom in tears and the father stoically standing beside her, they made an impassioned plea for whoever took their son to return him. I knew it was hopeless because I believed Jordan was dead. Eventually, someone would find his body. I watched most of the channels that I could, wanting to keep on top of any breakthroughs. The school fired Bateman, of course. And no other school or any other establishment would hire him. I didn't know what he was using for money, but it wouldn't last forever.

A week went by and it came time for me to move on. Normally, I liked to jump around and spread out my worksites, but this time I wanted to stay in the area and keep tabs on Bateman. I discovered another state park nearby needing volunteers, and I offered my services. It took me a day to clean up my campsite and hitch my truck to the Rockwood. I said goodbye to the other park hosts and drove to the next park to set up camp. Not much had happened, unless you watched the tabloid stations or similar shock jock stations. They made it sound like information, already mentioned several days before, was a fresh discovery. Totally useless after first reported.

I began tracking a new predator. To make it easier on myself, I revisited the predator websites and used my new zip code. I wondered if the police could track your activity on the net. The movies and books sensationalized the powers of the police and Homeland Security to unheard of levels, so I wasn't sure if they could or couldn't. I wasn't too concerned at this point because this website was getting hundreds of thousands of hits per week. I doubted even a super police state could track them all down. Still, after this I'd have to see about making myself a little more obscure.

Myron Stone was my next target. He lived outside of town in an older ranch style home and turned out to be an easy watch. Trees obscured his house from the road, and I could park my car without him or others in the neighborhood seeing it. Myron had a big yard, which isolated his house even more. Plus, he liked to keep his window blinds open. With a decent pair of binoculars, I could see inside every room on this side of his house. I kept watch when I could over the next several days.

On the surface, Myron seemed a normal person. However, his rap sheet was lengthy on child sexual abuse charges. He did some time a while back and appeared to be almost a model citizen since then. He was registered as a sex offender all right and proper, and I even saw a police officer visit his house. Because Myron had paid his debt to society the police would need a pretty good reason to search his house without a search warrant. Without probable cause, they weren't going to get one.

Something didn't seem right to me. From what I read earlier, rehabilitation, while possible, was unlikely in the case of a serial child rapist. What I saw here was just too neat. Too clean. Myron worked at a grocery store as a cashier on a predictable schedule. While I was contemplating his schedule, it occurred to me I could use this to my advantage.

The next time Myron left for work I broke into his house. Myron was neat as a pin. The kitchen was enormous, with a white tile floor and oak veneer cupboards. A fair amount of counter space with a stove, refrigerator, and dishwasher in the traditional triangle pattern for best use. The countertop also contained a microwave, a coffee pot, and a toaster.

Pretty much standard fare. No dishes in the sink, everything put away in the cupboard. And the countertops were clean, with a cutting board next to the double sink. Within the cupboards were dishes, dry and canned goods, breakfast cereal, the usual. The refrigerator had its milk, eggs, butter, some diet soda, vegetables, and the like. The freezer was stuffed with frozen things. Myron had everything meticulously organized. This extreme attention to detail added to my suspicions that Myron wasn't all he seemed. This was all just too pat.

Down the hall, the first bedroom I saw was an office of sorts. A computer and monitor sat on the desk, with papers here and there. Everything in the office was where it belonged. No waste, no mess. It creeped me out, so I looked in the master bedroom and bathroom as well. Again, everything was super neat. The bed made, the pillows and comforter precisely placed. In the bathroom, the bathing products lined up like little soldiers. His cordless toothbrush stood next to a ceramic cup within which he had a tube of toothpaste, partially squeezed. Nothing obvious jumped out at me, other than the creep factor, so I went back to the computer. I was a little nervous about doing this, but told myself it would be hours before Myron came back.

I pulled on a pair of plastic gloves. These were much like the ones used in crime stories I watched on TV, and depressed the on switch to the computer, and waited for it to boot. I could see he had a sophisticated mesh Wi-Fi network system, so the speed should be decent. It looked like a newer computer as well, so the processor should be fast too. Surprisingly, this computer was not password protected. The first thing I did was log onto the Internet and select view Internet history. Nothing there; completely plain Jane. His history was about the news, games, a recipe site, utterly bland. Blech. Nothing to see here.

A bell went off in my head as I thought this through. *Myron was on probation. The police could visit his home anytime and conduct a search throughout the house if they felt it warranted. The search would include his computer, of course. So he kept innocuous stuff on it to fool the cops. The cops were smart, I'm sure, and most likely knew he was up to something, but they couldn't completely toss his house without probable cause.* With their workload, I imagined a search that became more and more lax as time went by and nothing turned up.

I got up from the computer and started looking around more closely. The stories my wife told me about predators unable to be rehabilitated came to mind. These monsters would always feel the urge to exploit their victims, either sexually or through physical violence. I could feel something was going on. With that in mind, I began a very slow, studious examination of the house. I pulled open all the drawers in the computer desk, feeling under the drawers, searching for something taped on the underside. Next, I looked around in the shelving that held books and knick-knacks, just in case he was storing data on a stick. But I felt I was looking for a laptop. That made more sense than a second desktop machine or removable drive. The more I thought about it, the more convinced I became. A laptop is more convenient and much easier to hide. I searched both bedrooms and found nothing. After looking through the entire house; office, bedroom, laundry room, bathroom, living room, and garage, I still came up empty. *Where was the laptop?* I slowed way down and started over again. *If I were Myron, where would I hide a laptop?* I had to think like Myron. I was a convicted felon for child molestation. If they caught me with child pornography or on a child pornography website, I would go to jail for a long time. Plus, I'd probably get the shit beat out of me in jail, maybe worse. Prison inmates don't like people who hurt young children. I wouldn't last a week in prison, especially as I was a repeat offender.

So, if I couldn't help myself, and I just had to have a stash to look at, where would I put a laptop so the cops couldn't find it without probable cause? I surveyed the living room, noting every piece of furniture and its positioning. The walls. Could Myron have built some sort of secret panel behind which he could store a laptop? What about the pictures on the walls I looked at? Nothing. I didn't see a place a cop wouldn't think of. I moved into the bedroom. It contained a double bed, a nightstand, a lamp, and various miscellaneous items. I looked in the closet and saw the laundry hamper. It was an odd place for the hamper. I would have kept it in the bathroom. Something drew me to the hamper. I lifted the lid and wrinkled my nose at the used laundry smell. It seemed like Myron may not be as clean as he could be. I found a coat hanger and used it to probe the bottom of the hamper. The hanger hit something hard.

At first, I thought I hit the bottom of the hamper, but it didn't sound right. I reached into the bottom. My hand felt something and I pulled it up. Jackpot! In my hands was the suspected laptop. The hamper was an excellent spot, especially with the laptop buried down at the bottom and smelly clothing items on top of it. A police officer would think twice before going through someone else's dirty laundry if he didn't have a reason to. I brought the laptop out to the dining room table and opened it up. It looked like a pretty new unit. I pushed the on button and waited. To my surprise, no password was required here either. It automatically logged itself onto the Internet, and into a default location. My stomach lurched when I saw the images on display.

The default location was a child porno site with pictures and mini videos plastered all over it. It was all I could do to keep from throwing up. Everything I needed was right here. Myron wasn't cured of anything. He would strike again.

Chapter 15

I replaced everything as it was and crept out of the house, through the back door. My mind was in turmoil. *What was I going to do with this information? I could go to the police, but what if they did nothing? If I told them where the laptop could be found, what would they do with Myron? Put him back in jail? Jail was too good for him. He had hurt little children and would go on hurting them. I couldn't let that happen.* I stopped walking toward my car and turned back toward his house. Once back inside, I looked around the kitchen, noticing for the first time it used natural gas. I found the pilot light for the stove and blew it out. Beside the stove was the valve for adjusting the gas. I turned it up to full, waited to hear the hiss of escaping gas, then went back to my truck and drove home.

CHAPTER 16

Hours later, Myron Stone came home from work, using his remote to open the garage door, and then pulled in. He stopped at the door between the garage and house to put his key in the lock. As he stepped into the kitchen, the smell of gas didn't register with him before he flipped the light switch. After that, it didn't matter.

The local evening news and the papers the next day were full of the incredible explosion that rocked the Looking Glass Hill neighborhood the night before. Myron Stone was the victim of a gas explosion in his home. The suspected cause being the pilot light on the stove. The stove, which was an older model, had a pilot light that had blown out, a common problem. Myron's house and himself were destroyed after the fire department concluded he turned on the light switch, which ignited the gas. The news swiftly recapped the evening the firefighters spent battling the blaze, and then they went on to the next local event.

I was very pleased to hear about this and the fact that foul play was not a topic of discussion, at least on the evening news. The thrill of at last taking action, instead of standing on the sidelines, filled me with such joy and happiness I almost cried.

The gas trick was a lucky break for me, but had also revealed to me how I wanted to spend the rest of my life. I wouldn't wait for the police to act. I would determine if the target was still active. If so, I would end them. I would make it look like an accident, if possible, but I wouldn't let that stop me. In the few months left to me, I would make a difference in this world of shit and rid it of some of the vilest scum that walked the earth. I had no qualms, and I anticipated where this would likely lead. But I was ready. I would kill the bastards. As many as I could, until they caught me, I would kill the bastards. I was not afraid. I was ready.

Chapter 17

(One year later)

I swept the floor of yurt C-9, dumping the waste into the unit's trashcan. Then I took the plastic bag from the waste can and tossed it into the back of the motorized golf cart we used to drive around the campsites. Following up with a quick once over, I shut the door, locked it, and the unit was ready for occupancy once again. This was my last unit for the day, and I was ready to sit down and take it easy.

I got into the golf cart and started the engine. Some carts these days were electric, but today I was using one of the older models that ran on propane. It reminded me of my younger days in security at a major manufacturer when I did parking lot traffic.

Easing out the clutch, I started forward and headed down the asphalt path toward my RV space. On the way, I passed a few retirees like me who waved as I passed. Some of these people I had known for years, but I purposely kept my distance from them in recent months. The why was obvious. After a little nap and some follow up research, I planned to leave for a while and hunt down another sick monster. I could hardly play a game of bridge and suddenly leave, saying "Excuse me, I have to go murder another child sex offender." It just wouldn't be right. I had some regrets, sure, but what I was doing felt so right it negated any desire to go back to the way I was.

So far, I had been lucky. Not only with sixteen meticulously devised terminations that appeared to be accidents, but also with the cancer.

According to the doctors here, my cancer was in remission. None of them knew how long the remission would last. But I viewed each day as a windfall. I preceded each termination I performed with research into the target selected. I often went through their garbage and broke into their homes when the opportunity presented itself. If the evidence was there, I arranged an accident. If the evidence wasn't there, I left them in the database I was building for further study. Periodically, I swung back in my searches to keep up to date on their activities. So far, no one had been arrested, but you never knew.

Eventually, the statistics would catch up with me. I was a bit surprised it hadn't happened already. The police these days now had all kinds of crime databases to help them. As soon as an officer put the right information together, a pattern of accidents related to sex offenders would emerge. It wouldn't be long after that the police knew a serial killer was on the loose. Regardless of who the killer was hunting, they would track me down. I tried to be as careful as possible, but my time would come.

This afternoon, I was going after Johnny Fields, another monster from my list of monsters. Johnny was yet another local scumbag wandering the streets in search of prey. I caught him eying a nine-year-old girl at the grocery store and swore I'd punch his ticket before he hurt another person. His past police record and current behavior showed he wanted to hurt that little girl, despite no proof in his home or garbage. Whatever his plans were, it was pitiful how transparent he appeared to me.

That afternoon I watched him working at one of the local gas station mini marts that were the craze these days. He wore faded blue denim jeans and a gray polo shirt, white socks with tennis shoes. He serviced the cars quickly and always said thank you to the customer. At 5 pm, his shift was over. After washing his hands in the station's bathroom, Johnny jumped into his blue Toyota Prius and headed down the street to his house. Perfect.

I followed him from a discreet distance, surprised that he didn't turn off toward his home as I expected. *Where was he going?* He drove out of town, turning down an old dirt road I would have missed if I hadn't seen him turn in. A high arborvitae hedge shielded the road from the cross street. *What the hell was he up to*? I kept asking myself, pulling over to the side of the road. This was extremely suspicious. Obviously, I couldn't follow him down the road, so I drove a little way past and turned around a bend where my truck would be out of sight from the driveway.

I made my way back to the side road and surveyed the landscape. Deciduous and evergreen trees were everywhere. Stepping through the undergrowth, I hoped that whatever sat back here wasn't too far. Johnny wasn't in sight. I needed to know where he was so as not to bump into him or reveal my location. For all I knew, he might have a gun. Someone could construe me as a trespasser depending on whose property this turned out to be, and what Johnny boy was up to in it. After a few minutes of stumbling amongst the underbrush, I changed my mind and walked closer to the road but parallel to it, keeping to the trees as much as possible.

I trudged a long way, until at last I spotted a reflection in the distance, and soon after a small house appeared. Although it seemed deserted, I knew it wasn't. *Uh oh, this doesn't look good,* I thought to myself. Things were maybe beginning to make sense. Maybe nothing was found at his house because all his shit was here.

While waiting, I looked at the house. The cottage home was an older model, built in the style of the forties. Sheer curtains covered the windows and I could see the tops of the basement windows without curtains peering out from the foundation. The grass was high around the place, and moss was on the roof in thick clumps. It appeared no one lived here. Wait! That was untrue. A shadow passed by one of the kitchen windows. I assumed it was Johnny. I moved forward from tree to tree as quickly as I dared, not a hundred percent positive John couldn't see me but impatient to wait any longer. Reaching the side of the house, I crouched beneath the living room window. Presently I heard footsteps coming from stairs inside the house. A door opened, and then shut. Johnny must have gone into the basement, but now was on the main floor again. There must be hardwood floors inside because I could hear him walking around. My original plan was to go to Johnny's home and kill him there, but this seemed to be a prime opportunity to just make Johnny disappear. I eased toward the back of the house, looking for the back door. I peered through the window into the kitchen. Johnny wasn't there.

"What the fuck do you think you're doin'?" a voice said behind me.

My stomach clenched. *Shit, now I'm in for it. What do I say to him?* I spun around and Johnny stood there, a 9mm Glock 19 in his hands. I looked at the gun, then back at him. "Ya know, Johnny, it's a violation of your probation for you to have a gun."

"Fuck you. I said, what the fuck do you think you're doin' on my property?"

"Your property?" I said, stalling so I could think. "This is your property?"

"It sure as fuck is, and I don't like you on it. You're trespassing. I could shoot you in self-defense," said Johnny.

"Well now, that's not exactly true, Johnny, especially here in Oregon. That only works if I'm inside the house, and I have a weapon to threaten you with. Right now, if you kill me, you'll go back to jail because it would be murder. Now, instead of your pointing that gun at me, why don't we go inside and discuss it?" While talking, I edged my way toward him. Johnny was jittery. He might very well shoot me, regardless of what I was telling him.

"I don't want to go inside," Johnny said. "Maybe I'll just shoot you and take my chances." I inched forward a little more. Almost there. I don't think Johnny really wanted to shoot me. He just didn't realize that I really wanted to kill him.

"Why don't you just call the cops and have them arrest me?" That seemed to bother him. He clearly didn't want to go in the house with me, or get a visit from the cops, for that matter. What was in there he didn't want anyone to see? I decided to push it. I stepped toward the back door. "Here, let's go inside and we can wait for them." I opened the back door and stepped inside. With more speed than I thought possible, Johnny appeared behind me, obviously nervous about something.

"Hey," he said. "I've changed my mind. I–I won't press charges if you just leave. Now. Otherwise..." He brandished the pistol I didn't think he had the guts to use. I had anticipated this. As soon as the arc of the barrel swung past me and pointed at the wall, I rushed him, knocking him to the floor. I grabbed for the gun and we fought over it, both with desperation in our eyes. Although I was years older than Johnny, I outweighed him by 30 pounds, plus I knew a few dirty tricks. Quickly, I overpowered him and slugged him a few times to take the fight out of him. He finally went limp and began crying. I picked him up and set him in a kitchen chair. With the Glock trained on him, I searched through the kitchen drawers until I found some twine which I used to tie his hands and feet to the chair. Finally, I could relax. I pulled a chair in front of Johnny and sat down.

"So, Johnny, what are you hiding that you don't want the cops or me to see? Shall I go find out?" Johnny had a defeated, troubled expression, but enough fight in him to tell me to go to hell.

"Well, I might just do that, but I'm sure you'll be there before me." I smiled at him, tilting my head slightly to one side. "Don't go anywhere. I'm going to take a look around." I stood up from the chair and began going from room to room. Fancy drapes and small tables decorated the living room, and the house was tastefully furnished. The kitchen, where we were, was small, but a breakfast nook added depth and warmth to the area. It had three bedrooms, the master bedroom downstairs and the other two upstairs, and a bathroom on each floor. Upstairs wasn't much to see. A couple of beds and dressers. Nothing remarkable. I came back down the stairs and checked on Johnny. He was where I'd left him, his head down.

Then I opened the basement door. I could tell something wasn't right immediately. The place smelled wrong. I turned the light on over the stairs and headed down. The basement was unfinished. I saw nothing down here at first, then I noticed a section walled off from the rest of the basement. It didn't feel right and the hairs on my neck stood up. I was getting a horrible feeling. In the movies, this would be where the ominous music started and increase in intensity the closer I got to the plywood door, set in the walled off section. I took a breath, then turned the knob. The door swung inward and once opened, confirmed everything I ever imagined about the monster Johnny Fields. A filthy, bloodstained, queen sized bed lay on the floor at one end of the room. Near it, on a nightstand, lay tape, scissors, rope, a screwdriver, and a lighter. More was there, but I wasn't paying attention after that. In one corner, children's clothes hung from the ceiling, either trophies from victims or some other reason I couldn't figure out. A movie camera sat on a tripod near the foot of the bed, the lens pointed toward the mattress. What occurred in this room was glaringly apparent, and I felt nauseated just being in the vacant room. Thank God the room was empty. But something was still not right. If he collected trophies, that meant…

I walked back up the stairs. Johnny was struggling to get free, but I had wound that twine several times and made it tight. He failed to get loose. And now it was too late.

"Where are they, Johnny?" I asked. He looked up at me, a little scared.

"Where is who?" he asked. I pulled the gun I had taken from him in our scuffle from my pocket and shot him in the leg. My shot missed the bone, but blood spurted as he started screaming.

"Johnny, where are they? Tell me or by God, I'll use every last bullet on you, but leave you alive so you can bleed to death in agony. WHERE ARE THE DAMN CHILDREN?" Johnny looked up from staring at the blood pouring out of a hole in his leg, pain in his eyes and tears on his face. "I don't know," he said. My eyes widened as I got angrier and I shot him in the other leg.

"Don't give me that shit! You know what I found down there! Your private little torture chamber! You are one sick bastard. Tell me where the bodies are and I'll take you to jail so you can get fixed up. You'll never walk straight again, but that's what you get for not telling me the truth. WHERE ARE THEY?" I shouted the last at him and pointed the gun at his groin and my finger starting pulling the trigger. He saw the angle of the gun.

"Wait, wait, don't shoot me again, please." He hung his head in shame. "They're out in back by the trees. They're out in back by the trees. I didn't mean to do it. I couldn't help myself." Johnny started sobbing. I lowered the gun.

"Where's a shovel?" I asked. "Where's a goddamn shovel?"

"Out in the garage against the back wall. Please don't hurt me anymore.

Please. I'm in so much pain." I left him moaning and went out to the garage, looking for a shovel. Walking back to the trees at the far end of his back property, I could see mounds of earth slowly settling out. I chose one and started digging cautiously. In five minutes I found the body of a little seven-year-old girl. I looked at her little hand and cried. It was so small. Then, I covered her back up so the animals wouldn't get her and walked back to the house. Johnny was still there, moaning and crying

"Mercy, have mercy." He cried. I walked up to him and put the barrel of the Glock against his forehead.

"This is the only mercy you'll get from me, you sick fuck," I said and pulled the trigger. Johnny's head snapped back as the back of his head splattered against the kitchen wall.

On the way home, I stopped by a pay phone, gave the police the address of the house, and told them what they would find. Then I drove home, tears running down my cheeks the entire way.

Chapter 18

Mace Jackson leaned his head in the doorway of Lieutenant Anderson's office. "Hey, Lieutenant," he said, "This just came in. Some guy called in a child death site. Says he killed the guy who did it and the bodies are out back by the trees of this house about twenty miles from here."

Lieutenant Anderson looked up from his paperwork to stare at Jackson. "What?"

"I'm saying we got a multiple homicide with children and the perp was executed by a third party." Mace looked excited, his eyes bright as he relayed the next news to Anderson. "Hey Lieutenant, get this. It was Johnny Fields." The name caused Anderson's eyes to widen, and he stood up. Field's name was a name he knew well. The sex offender. The pedophile. Something tickled his brain about this, but he couldn't quite put his finger on it. Something about him being a pedophile -. He couldn't quite get a hold of the thought. Oh well, it would come to him sooner or later. Anderson grabbed his jacket.

"Let's go," he said.

By the time Anderson arrived, they had cordoned the area off with yellow crime scene tape and forensics was there. Inside the house, Johnny sat, tied to a wooden chair in the center of the kitchen with a hole in his head, as dead as you could get. Blood had pooled beneath him and spread across the tile floor. The coroner was examining the body. Death was pretty self-explanatory. Anderson made his way to the back of the house and stepped out onto the porch. In the backyard several officers were working the site, collecting evidence and marking where they found it. One plainclothes detective came toward him. Anderson recognized Ray Bliss. Ray was a seasoned veteran of the force, but even he had a sad face. The surrounding aura was palpable.

"Afternoon, Lieutenant," he stated, shaking hands with Anderson. "We've got quite a crime scene here. Looks like the tip was pretty accurate. There's the dead guy in the kitchen, plus we have several bodies out here at the tree line. It's pretty gruesome. These are all children, between six and ten. It will be up to forensics and the Medical Examiner to determine how they were killed, as some of them show signs of strangulation. I don't know when I've seen such a mess."

"Show me," said Anderson. For a second, Bliss seemed reluctant to take the Lieutenant back, but he shrugged his shoulders and led them to the trees. Several officers still dug in the earth, but four bodies lay on tarps upon the grass, pulled from shallow graves. It looked like Johnny, if he was the killer, had covered the bodies with lime to reduce the smell and accelerate the decomposition process. At least, that was Lieutenant Anderson's guess. The killer methodically planned these murders well in advance. Many clues abounded here. The case appeared cut and dry. From the Johnny Fields perspective, that is. But who was the guy that killed Johnny and called the cops? That's what Anderson wanted to know. Who was that guy? Anderson looked around until he spotted Mace.

"Mace, who took the call for this? Meyers?" Jackson thought for a moment.

"No, it wasn't Meyers. He's on vacation. It was Peterson. You know, Todd Peterson. "

"Get him on the phone. Tell him to make himself available for when we get back. I want to talk to him about this phone tip he got."

"You got it," said Jackson, heading towards the car. He sat on the driver's side of the car and keyed into headquarters, asking for Peterson. Moments later, he was back. "Todd says no problem. He's got some paperwork to do before he hits the street. He'll wait for you and then go out."

"Loverly," said Anderson. "Let's wrap our part up and go have a chat with Peterson. There's something familiar about this. I can't place it yet, but I will."

CHAPTER 19

It took me a couple days to recover from Mr. Fields. I didn't expect to find bodies. I just wanted to stop *him* permanently. But that young girl's hand, poking up through the dirt, was too much.

The good news was the incident strengthened my resolve to continue and wipe out these freaks of nature. The bad news was I originally planned to make it all look like an accident. Not only had I failed in that, I called the police and told them where to find Johnny and the children's bodies. For what I was trying to accomplish, that was a big mistake. It drew unwanted attention to me. Still, the death rate for the area was climbing. It wouldn't be long before the police realized what they had on their hands. What they did with that information would be interesting to discover.

The lieutenant I spoke with originally had showed up at the murder scene. I saw him on the eleven o'clock news and finally put a face to a name. He looked fit in his uniform. Dark hair, bright piercing eyes and a somewhat too sharp nose, thin lips. He appeared confident, in a bored sort of way. It made me see him as a tired, Columbo like character who plodded through the investigation and eventually came up with the killer every time. Maybe he would catch up with me, maybe not. Today's actions hadn't improved my chances for a long-term vendetta, that's for sure.

I finished watching the news and headed to bed, still drained from yesterday and feeling a little feverish. I wanted to take some acetaminophen and go to sleep. Fuck the rest of the world. After using the parks facilities and returning to the trailer, I pulled out my pillbox and shook out the selected pills for the evening. Metformin for diabetes, Lisinopril for blood pressure and to protect the kidneys, Simvastatin for high cholesterol, a low dose aspirin to thin the blood, and two giant calcium pills. I surveyed the selection in my palm with disgust. This was the price of old age. Pills that let you live longer, yet no change in the living environment. On the other hand, the pills reduced the effects of diabetes and other ailments, but their side effects weren't so great either. The Lisinopril made me dizzy if I stayed bent over too long or stood up too fast, while the Simvastatin made my joints ache if I wasn't careful. The Metformin made me constipated. All these side effects from pills and medicine that were meant to make me feel better. Wonderful.

Well, shit. I might as well take them and get it over with. I flipped the pills into my mouth all at once and drank the glass of water that sat on the nightstand. Finished, I rolled into bed, pulled the covers up around me, and grabbed the current book I was reading. It was some near future war story involving the Russians. Fast-paced, which kept me reading it. After a few chapters, I laid the book down, turned out the lamp, and rolled over to sleep. Tomorrow would be another day. My nightmare dream did not appear.

Chapter 20

Back at the office, Anderson looked at the notes he took during his discussion with Johnson. According to Johnson, the guy who called the station sounded incredibly upset. His voice shaking, he said he had killed some child predator out on Squire Road at some house, and that bodies of children were buried in the back by the trees. Then he hung up the phone. The call originated from a pay phone about two miles from the site. At least they had something. But the caller hung up before anyone could record the call. Therefore, they couldn't perform voice analysis or trace the call. He had a crew combing the house and surrounding area for clues, checking for some house cameras that may have caught something, but he wasn't optimistic.

Not much to go on, I'll admit, he thought to himself. It's too bad. On the one hand, I'd like to shake his hand for getting rid of scum like Johnny. On the other, it's never good to have vigilante justice metered out by civilians. They were breaking the law and needed to be stopped. He punched the retractor on his pen quickly over and over as he thought. Click. Click. Click. There's something about this case. Something I'm not seeing yet. Click. Click. Click. Shit, he wasn't going to solve it today. "Mace! Get your ass in here. We need to talk about what we have on that rape case over by the college."

And with that, he dismissed the Johnny Fields case from his mind. At least for the time being.

Chapter 21

Molly lived in a three bedroom, older ranch style home in a rather tranquil neighborhood. The house included a master and regular baths, three bedrooms and a double car garage, along with the standard kitchen, dining room, and living room. The house was gas heated and air-conditioned. Most of the yard was flat, with more yard in the back than in the front. A six foot wooden fence surrounded the back, while a four foot high, white picket fence encircled the front, complete with a small gate.

A concrete path led from the gate up to the front of the house to a covered porch where a small gabled overhead sheltered a person from most of the rain that was a mainstay in Oregon. The house was white with a light blue trim.

Molly was twelve the first time her stepfather touched her. He married her mother a few years back, and the family settled into a routine for several years before Molly found her step dad looking at her in a way she didn't like. Their relationship had been normal enough. She barely knew her biological father. He died in some worthless car accident on the way home from work. Her mother, inconsolable at first, finally pulled herself together and sought to keep food on the table and a roof over their head. It had been hard. She found work at a high-tech company manufacturing electronics. She grabbed overtime anytime she could and Molly often stayed with one of mom's friends when she worked Saturdays. Mom dated occasionally, but nothing seemed permanent until Barry.

Barry was a guy her mom knew from work, and they started talking at lunchtime. They developed a rapport and one day he asked her out. After a few dates, Barry started coming over for dinner once or twice a week. Molly liked him well enough. By then her body began to develop, with hair growing where hair hadn't grown before and swellings on her chest. She had her first period. She knew what was happening. Her mother talked to her about puberty and Molly was eager to enter that phase and become a young woman. On the other hand, she still liked to spend time in her bedroom, watching TV, texting on her cell phone to her girlfriends for hours about boys and listening to music. She still played with her dolls occasionally.

Mom and Barry were together about five years when Barry said something to her while her mom was in the kitchen doing dishes after dinner. Barry and Molly were in the living room, watching TV.

"Well," Barry said, striking up a conversation. "Looks like we're becoming a little woman, aren't we?" Molly blushed deeply and crossed her arms over her chest.

"I don't know what you mean," she mumbled.

"Oh, of course you do, sweetheart. I bet the boys have been looking at you, haven't they?" The truth of his statement made her blush even more.

"Please don't talk to me like that. It's not right," she whimpered. Barry chuckled and put his hand on her shoulder.

"It's alright, pumpkin, I understand. But you should know, someday you are going to be a very beautiful young woman and men are going to look at you in strange ways." After that, she observed him eyeing her similarly to the boys at school, causing her to feel self-conscious. She thought about telling her mom what Barry had said, but did nothing, brushing it off as a onetime thing. Over the next few weeks, however, she caught him looking at her as though he were undressing her with his eyes. She took to avoiding him where she could, and wouldn't look at him at all unless absolutely necessary. Her mother picked up on it, but attributed the withdrawal as the typical teenage shyness stage. However, to her credit, she did try to reach Molly.

"Molly, how come you didn't want Barry to take you to the store?"

She asked one day. “He was just trying to be nice.”

“I don’t know,” Molly said evasively. “I just wanted to walk. There wasn’t that much to get and bring home.” Her mom laughed at her daughter.

“Well, honey, next time, let him drive you. It would make me feel better if you’re with someone safe.” Molly shrugged her shoulders, sidling by her mom for the front door.

“I don’t know, mom, I have to think about it.” The screen door slammed behind her as she left the house.

“Hmm,” her mother said. “I wonder what’s got into her?”

“Beats me,” said Barry, sitting on the couch. “Maybe I pissed her off somehow, I dunno know.” He kept his private thoughts to himself.

Molly asked some of her friends about it at school. “He’s always staring at my boobs,” she confided to Janice, her best friend. They sat outside at a picnic table, apart from the other students, during the school lunch break. She felt better about talking more freely this way. “He’s tried to see me in the shower and when I’m walking to my bedroom in a towel. I don’t know what to do.”

Janice, a serious, pragmatic blonde with a perpetual ponytail, sat with a turkey sandwich in her hand. “Have you said something to your mom?” she asked. Molly shook her head, looking down at the bench seat, unable to look Janice in the eyes.

“No, I just can’t bring myself to say anything. Nothing’s really happened yet. I just feel uncomfortable around him.”

“Well,” Janice began. “If it were me, I would either confront him about it or say something to my mom. She wouldn’t stand for it and kick the bastard out. That’s what you need to do.” Molly wasn’t sure she should do that. It was Barry’s money that helped pay the bills, and her mom made sure she understood that and to treat Barry with respect. Molly wasn’t sure they could make it if he were to leave.

“I don’t know, Janice. It’s so hard to know the right thing to do.” The school bell rang, and the girls tossed their food packaging into a nearby garbage can, picked up their books, and wandered off to class.

Molly said nothing to her mother, and didn't confront Barry. Barry continued to sneak peeks at her whenever he could and Molly just accepted it until a couple of weeks later, everything changed.

Chapter 22

Mom," Molly pleaded, tears in her eyes. "Please don't go. I don't want to be alone!" Her mother looked at her, a small smile on her face.

"Alone? You're not alone. Barry's going to be right here. Nothing's going to happen to you."

"But mom, I don't like the way he looks at me. He's always staring at my chest."

"Now that's just plain silly," her mother said, laughing dismissively. "He's just goofing around. Just ignore him." Molly stood by the door, shoulders drooping despondently.

"Mom, please–" she started. Molly's mother's smile disappeared, and she stood firmly at the door, keys in hand, her jacket folded over one arm. Barry had already placed her suitcase in the car.

"Stop it, young lady, right now! I'll have no more of this. You're acting like you're six years old. I'm going to be gone just for a couple of days for this training class. I'm sorry it's not closer, but that's the way it is." Her face softened. "Honey, with this training, I'll get to be a level III technician and get a raise. We need that money. Now that's final." She leaned over and gave Molly a peck on the cheek and opened the door to the garage. She walked around to the driver's side, tossed her jacket onto the passenger seat, then deposited herself behind the steering wheel, fastening her seat belt. As she started the car, she pressed the remote garage door unit as the door rose. She backed out waving at Molly watching from the door, pulled out into the street and, with no more preamble, drove off. Molly stayed at the door, watching her mom's car until it vanished down the street. She felt helpless and dreaded being alone with her stepdad.

She pushed off the doorframe and came back into the living room, arms wrapped around herself, intending to make a beeline straight to her bedroom and shut the door.

"Molly."

Molly froze in mid step. Barry's voice had changed. It was stronger, more forceful, commanding. Intimidating, evil. She had never heard it before, and it made her blood run cold.

"Molly, come here. Sit beside me, girl." Barry said. "This is our first chance to get to know each other better. Come over here."

Molly trudged toward the couch where Barry sat, her body stiff. She sat down at the far end of the couch from Barry, who grinned, his teeth gleaming. She once thought Barry had a very engaging, charming smile, but now it looked hideous, too bright and shined wetly. How had she never seen that before? She was suddenly horribly conscious of her dress. She wore a short dress patterned with flowers, reaching a few inches above her knees. Her legs were bare, except for multi-colored socks she liked to wear. Underneath the dress, she wore a slip, bra, and panties. Barry looked relaxed against the corner of the couch, supported by the back and the arm. He reminded her of an enormous spider she once saw, sitting on its web, waiting for its next meal.

"Now look, Molly." Barry started said. "If we are going to know each other better, you'll have to be closer than that. Come closer." Molly looked down at her knees, shaking her head in short, swift arcs. Barry sat up and moved closer to her, so close their legs touched. Molly tried to press further into the couch, away from him, but there wasn't any place to go. "Well," Barry said. "If you won't come to me, I guess I'll come to you. Now, isn't this better?"

Molly didn't answer, just kept looking at her knees. Barry reached out to touch her hair, and she cringed away from him.

"Please," she pleaded. "Please don't do this." A tear ran down her face. Barry didn't appear to notice.

"Please don't do what, Molly? I just want to know you." He leaned in as though to kiss her, but she jumped up and ran to her room, locking the door behind her. “Please! Please, just leave me alone!” she cried. She listened intently at the door, but heard nothing from the other side. She sat down on her bed and started to cry. Suddenly, she heard noises at the door, but before she could move to block the door, it swung open. Molly’s door locked but featured a small hole in the center, making it possible for someone to open it from the outside if it was locked by mistake. All it took was a small, flat-bladed screwdriver, which Barry held in his hand. Insert, twist, and he was in her room. Molly was so scared she couldn’t breathe, couldn’t gather a breath to scream before Barry sauntered over to the bed towering above her. His smile was malicious as he reached down for her.

“Make any noise or tell your mother and I will hurt both of you badly. This isn’t my first rodeo, bitch. And I know how to keep little sluts like you quiet.”

As he forced her back onto the bed, the bedroom door slowly closed with a soft click.

CHAPTER 23

Molly lay cowering on the mattress, terrified of her abductor's return. She was in perpetual darkness, except for the crack of light seeping through under the door. She was grateful for the light yet terrified of it, because shadows within it would announce his return to her and she desperately did not want him to return. Ever. Especially after the last time when he hurt her so deeply. He must be getting over his need for her. His urges were becoming more brutal, violent.

But he was climaxing less often, as though he were bored. Soon he would become so violent that in his rage he would probably beat her to death. That would be a relief. To be beyond all this pain. This misery. This sorrow. She turned and buried her face into the filthy pillow beneath her head. God, I wish I were dead! She moaned softly to herself. At least then it would all be over.

CHAPTER 24

I woke up finally, able to face the day. Lately I stumbled through my cleanings, barely managing to do so only so I could keep my rental space. But my mind was elsewhere and I at last snapped back to reality. The sun was shining; the birds were chirping, and the police had yet to knock on my door. I breathed a sigh of relief. Climbing out of bed, I fixed a light breakfast, then went to the park facilities to shower and shave. After that, I felt somewhat refreshed and able to look at the new day with a clear head.

It was obvious I needed to get out of the area, for sure. Get away from the memories of the last few days and seek fresh territory. Luckily, my time was near up, so leaving wouldn't cause a comment that an investigative cop might pick up. A detective was sure to visit here, eventually. Although the press was given little information, someone would eventually connect the dots and start the investigation. Until then, everything had to appear normal. Nevertheless, I needed to alter my routine somewhat and relocate, possibly to a completely different state. Muddy up the evidence trail a bit. Yeah, that sounded like a great idea. It was too early to head home yet, to my house in McMinnville. I got on the computer and began researching state parks with full hookups in different states near me. I found a few, then finally one I could afford. Approaching Alicia, the park host, I told her I was leaving tomorrow. She was used to people with trailers and RVs getting a stick up their butt and leaving on a whim. I did myself, now and then, but not for quite a while. It was the wanderlust spirit in so many of us off the grid types. She raised her eyebrows a bit at my sudden notice but said little, just wished me the best and she'd look forward to my return.

Back at my trailer site, I picked up all the outside camping accessories, packing them in their allotted places within the trailer and the truck. If you did it right, it was amazing how much gear you could stuff in these trailers. And of course, the truck had lots of room too. With the capper for the truck bed attached, it made for even more room. Retracting the dish antenna and coiling up the hoses, all I had to do now was disconnect the power supply and do a sweep around the site for anything I had missed. Tomorrow I would raise the stabilizing jacks, hook up the truck and be on the way. I needed to be well rested for my drive, so I read a book in bed instead of watching TV for an hour. As I relaxed, my eyes got heavy, and I laid the book down, shut off the light, and went to sleep. My dream did not haunt me this time.

Early the following morning, I got up, made breakfast, and cleaned the dishes. After seeing to my hygiene needs, I was ready to get the hell out of there. I hooked up the trailer, then circled around the camp in a last sweep for anything missed. I climbed into the driver's seat of the truck and started the engine. It turned over smoothly, and I strapped on my seat belt and readjusted all the mirrors. I pulled out of the park, heading south on Highway 101, planning to work my way down to Reno via Grants Pass. I wasn't one hundred percent sure of the route, but my GPS device would get me there. Reno hadn't become too warm yet, merely in the seventies. But it was always busy, and a new face or rig wouldn't raise eyebrows. My idea was to stick it out near Reno for a while and then head north up into Idaho. I would come back down later through Washington, back into Oregon, and home. Once home, I could rest in my proper bed, relax among familiar surroundings, and plan my next venture into vigilante serial killing. In some ways, I was enjoying this. I actually started whistling as my rig roared down the highway.

CHAPTER 25

Holding his morning coffee, Mace Jackson stepped into his boss's office and planted himself in one of the chairs placed in front of the lieutenant's desk. Anderson looked up from his paperwork and scowled at him, waiting for the explanation of this intrusion. "Not too much to go on from that child killer slaying," Mace said. "No prints, no blood, the footprints in the grass too indistinct for any castings. No tire tracks. This guy is a genuine ghost, Lieutenant. No shells from the gun, so it was either a revolver or he picked up his shells after he was done, and took the gun with him. I've got men throughout the neighborhood talking with neighbors, searching areas for the gun and clues. This guy isn't stupid. We found traces of white powder on the phone, chair and shovel, which we both know means plastic gloves. This guy is slick. There's no doubt about that."

Anderson leaned forward in his chair. "This guy may be a ghost, but some aspects of this case seem amateurish, sensitive. He sounded awfully shook up when he called in, like he really cared about those kids. Killing Fields may have just been a knee jerk response to the violence."

Jackson raised his eyebrows. "If you ask me, putting a bullet through a person's head is a pretty big knee-jerk reaction. I know what you're saying, but I sure wish we had more leads."

"They'll come, just give it time. We're still in the early stages of the crime yet."

Jackson leaned forward from his chair. "Are we? Could this be something bigger we just haven't put together yet?"

"Maybe," said Anderson. "When you get a chance, put what you know into VICAP, see what you come up with."

"Will do. It'll be a couple of days yet. Mind if I let one of the interns put in the info?"

"Good idea. They need the experience anyway. Just make sure to check their work." Mace stood from his chair.

"Will do. Anything else?"

"No," said Anderson. "Not right now. Keep on those guys out at the site. They may come up with something yet."

After Jackson left, Anderson sat at his desk, pondering the elements of the case. He was eager to know how many bodies were found buried behind the house. Right now, they didn't even know who the house belonged to. Was there another reason Johnny picked that house other than its secluded location? Did it belong to relatives? Was it a vacation home of some city dweller? Who knew? Well, it was his job to find out. Give it another twenty-four hours and he knew some answers would start coming in.

Chapter 26

Back on Highway 101, I felt better. The memories of the past few days dimmed as I pulled away from town. Turning on the radio, I flipped to a local station I liked. The day wasn't half-bad, a little cloudy, but otherwise ok. The lack of rain gave me a boost in morale. Things were definitely looking up.

After a couple hours driving, I definitely felt less dirty from being in the same room with Johnny. I was glad he was dead. How many children did that fucking bastard kidnap and do whatever he did to them before I caught up with him? The house where I killed him might not be the only place he hid the bodies. I would never know for sure how many children died at the hands of Johnny Fields. I just knew there wouldn't be any more.

The first day I drove for about five hours, traveling a couple of hundred miles, then pulled into a truck stop late in the afternoon. When I climbed out of the truck to stretch my legs, a savory aroma filled the air, and I decided to eat in the diner after I freshened up. I used the restroom, then entered the diner and sat by the window. A moment later, a waitress in a non-descript uniform arrived with a menu and a glass of water.

"Hey there," she said with a big smile, placing the menu on the table in front of me. She was about five foot five, with bright blue eyes, twenty-four years old, maybe, with brown hair and a nice figure. I was old enough to be her father or even her grandfather, but I still noticed she was attractive. "Where are you coming from?" she asked.

"Oh, I've been driving a while on my way through California to visit friends in Palm Beach," I lied. "Haven't seen them in years." She looked at me with uninterested eyes.

"Hmmm, that sounds nice. Care for coffee?"

"Sure. Sounds wonderful."

"Be right back," she said, turning and walked back toward her beverage station. I opened the menu and scanned the contents. By the time she returned, I knew what I wanted and ordered a turkey club sandwich with a side of ranch dressing. The selection came with fries and I added a small house salad for a couple of bucks more. She took the menu from me, smiled, and moved to the next booth to help another customer. Later, when she returned with my order, I contemplated what the next actions of the police might be while I ate my sandwich.

By now, Lieutenant Anderson and his team would have uncovered the bodies at the back of the yard where I told them they could find the bodies. Johnny's death would be the first obvious murder I had committed. All the others I set up to appear as accidents. Jumping to another park the way I did should keep them confused for a while, but eventually there would be too many bodies to ignore. The case would get prioritized and one detective would get the assignment of pulling the case together. Once it was clear a serial killer was loose, they would add more resources to hunt down and apprehend the vigilante I had become. It wouldn't matter that the victims were monster child offenders. Funny, I thought. I didn't think of myself as a vigilante, just a person doing something to make things better in the world. Be that as it may, this project of mine would get tougher all the time until I was caught or killed. It was a time to move onward to safer waters.

Before I finished my meal, the waitress came back with my bill. "Say," I asked. "I'm exhausted. Is it ok if I spend the night here? I don't need a room. I have my trailer." The waitress nodded as she placed the bill on the table.

"Yeah, it only cost ten dollars and that includes use of the showers and breakfast tomorrow morning."

"Well, that sounds like a terrific deal," I said. "Who do I talk to?"

"Just go to the front desk and they'll set you up," the waitress said. I smiled at her as I reached for my wallet to pay the bill.

"Okay, thanks."

Having paid my bill plus tip, I stopped at the front desk and arranged to spend the night as the waitress suggested. After that, I walked back to the trailer and lowered the stabilizer jacks. It was early yet, four o'clock or so, but I was tired and just wanted to go to bed. I extended the antenna and stayed up long enough to see if any news about Johnny Fields had reached the media yet. Upon learning that there were no updates on Johnny Fields, I prepared for sleep and nestled between the cool sheets. In minutes, I was fast asleep.

The night passed without incident. I woke up feeling better than I had in a long time. After I showered, shaved, and had breakfast in the diner, I felt refreshed. I lowered the TV antenna, raised the jacks, then climbed into the truck. Betsy fired right up and I pulled up to a gasoline pump. Jumping out again, I filled the tank, climbed back in, and then slowly pulled my truck and trailer through the gas island. I was careful to watch my swing as I angled out of the parking lot and merged onto the Interstate 5, once again heading towards Nevada. It was a cool, crisp morning and the air smelled wonderful.

Chapter 27

With Barry molesting Molly whenever Molly's mother wasn't around, it wasn't long before Molly decided to run away. Clearly, her mother wasn't going to jeopardize her meal ticket, so things for Molly wouldn't change. She set up a weekend stay with Janice for that Friday. After dinner, she told her mother she was spending the weekend at Janice's house. Her mom and Barry sat on the couch, preparing for a night of TV or movies. Molly didn't really care. She didn't feel a part of their lives anymore. In her room, she filled her school backpack with as many clothes and toiletries as she could manage, changed into a pair of shorts with a T-shirt and tennis shoes. After saying goodbye, she quietly slipped out the door and walked down the street. Tears ran down her face as she made her way towards Janice's house, a lonely dog barking faintly in the distance.

It was late summer, so the weather wasn't bad at all. The night before, Molly texted Janice to discuss her options about what to do or where she should go. Janice was adamant Molly spend her first runaway night with her. For Janice, it wasn't so much Molly removing herself from a toxic situation as it was a dramatic adventure. After Molly reached her house, she and Janice had a quick conversation with Janice's mother. Then the girls went upstairs, and Molly quietly cried on Janice's bed while Janice rattled on about absolutely everything without really saying much of anything, oblivious to Molly and her feelings. But, after a while, Janice tuned in to how depressed Molly was with leaving her home and her mom and the two began talking earnestly about what Molly was going to do. Molly had saved money through babysitting around the neighborhood. She added to that with part of a stash found in her mother's closet one day. Molly wasn't snooping or looking to steal from her own mom, but she was looking for something to wear with a blouse she had on and stumbled on to the stash box. She didn't take all the money, just some to help her get by until she found a job. A couple of hundred dollars. Although she needed it, she felt guilty taking it. She told herself she would pay her mother back when she got settled. Molly also needed a new cell phone and number, because her current cell had one of those locater apps on it so her mother or police could track her movements. She couldn't very well stay hidden with that on her person. They talked far into the night until they were both exhausted, and each fell into slumber.

After breakfast the next morning, the girls convinced Janice's mother to drive them to the nearest mall, telling her they would take a bus back home when they were done shopping. Because of her limited funds, Molly could only window shop the blouses, pants, dresses, and shoes that surrounded them in virtually every store. At the mall, they finally made it to a cell phone kiosk where Molly purchased a new, no contract cell phone with a new number. The kiosk operator helped her transfer contact information and some apps she wanted to keep. But she could leave the locater app behind, so she was free. After she had the phone, Molly felt a sense of relief. If she needed to contact her mom, she would use someone else's phone or maybe a store phone.

The two girls then ate lunch at a fast-food hamburger place, made another trip through the mall to double check the clothes, then caught a bus back to Janice's house. Once home, they went to the kitchen, poured themselves some soda to drink from the refrigerator, then headed upstairs, more or less ignoring Janice's mother. If it wasn't for the horror that waited for Molly back at her house and how she was handling it, they would have been having a fun time. Molly was staying another night, and Janice's mom made them all dinner. Janice's mom noticed something was weighing on Molly's mind, but she refrained from asking. She had her own daughter to worry about.

After dinner and helping with the dishes, the second part of their master plan was developed. Molly would spend the night as planned, then, in the morning, she would walk to the bus depot and buy a ticket to somewhere other than here. Using Janice's computer, the girls looked at various cities or states Molly could ride to using public transportation. The best rates were for Tuesday. It looked like she would have to return home. Her best plan then would be to attend first period on Tuesday, so her attendance would get recorded.

After first period, she would board the bus and head for California. That would give her a day to get out of town and beyond Barry's reach. It wasn't her first choice, but in order to save money, it would have to do. Once in Los Angeles or Sacramento, she intended to get a job in retail, maybe in some fashion boutique. It would probably be minimum wage, but she felt certain she could get discounts on clothing.

Against her better judgement then, she returned home. But first, she and Janice stashed her clothes and things at Janice's where she could get to them.

As she walked up the driveway, Molly was relieved to see her mom's car parked in the garage. Entering the house, she announced she was home, and her mother appeared from the living room. A small look of concern crossed her face.

"Hello darling, I was getting worried about you. It's getting late. I tried to call your cell, but you didn't answer." Molly's face reddened at her oversight.

"Oh, sorry mom. My battery is dead. I forgot to take my charger over to Janice's." Molly's mom didn't seem too perturbed, just glad she was back.

"Well, it's a school night, so don't stay up too late tonight. Do you want something to eat?"

Molly nodded, as she was hungry, but she was visibly nervous. She had to ask. "Where's Barry?" Her mom, preoccupied with fixing dinner, was looking in the cupboard for something to fix for Molly to eat. Moving cans of soup and boxes of rice, beans, and cake mixes, she replied.

"Oh, he went over to Adam's house, over on Belmont. There's some game or something on the tv. Anyway, he won't be home until late, so it's just you and me tonight. After dinner, do you want to watch a movie or something?" Molly visibly relaxed. She wouldn't have to put up with that pervert tonight, which was fine with her.

"Sorry, mom. I've got some homework I forgot about that's due tomorrow." Molly's mom looked a little disappointed, but accepted the typical teenager attitude her daughter exhibited. "Suit yourself," she said. Molly could tell her mom was annoyed, and a little hurt. It was clear she felt her baby drifting away from her.

Dinner was nothing special, and after helping with the dishes, Molly walked down the hall to her bedroom. She was genuinely worn out. She and Janice had stayed up late talking about her plans, and she needed to get to bed early because of that. With Barry in the house, she was taking her showers at night so he wouldn't ogle her in her towel, which he truly liked to do. It gave her the creeps. After her shower, she combed her hair, brushed her teeth, and crawled into bed. Sleep eluded her for a while, but she finally succumbed to its embrace.

On Monday, she woke to the alarm, got up and dressed quickly. Creeping past her mom's bedroom, she went into the kitchen and opened the refrigerator to pour herself a glass of almond milk. Heading for the front door, she picked up a banana to complete her breakfast and then was on her way to the school bus stop. Janice was already there, waiting for her, eager to see her but not saying anything. She was clearly about to burst, barely able to contain herself. Molly gave her 'a settle down, what is wrong with you' look and Janice relaxed a bit. She needn't have bothered, as all the other kids ignored Janice, caught up in conversations with their own friends. The bus then arrived and all the students at the stop climbed aboard and found their seats. Janice and Molly sat together.

As the bus pulled away from the curve, Molly leaned over to whisper in Janice's ear. "Any problems getting to my stuff tomorrow morning?" Janice shook her head furtively.

"No," she said. "Shouldn't be any issues. Your duffel bag is still there." That made Molly feel a little better. At least that part of the plan was intact.

"We'll complete our plan tonight after dinner. I'll call you." Molly leaned back against the seat and blew out a gigantic sigh of air. She really didn't want to do this, but she couldn't say anything to her mother about

Barry molesting her, so there was little choice. She turned her head and looked out through the window at the landscape until their bus arrived at the school.

It was impossible for her to concentrate on her classes, and the day took forever. Finally, the bell rang for the end of seventh period and time for her to go home. She waited at the bus stop for Janice and together they rode the bus, quietly going over her plan, trying to make sure everything was in place.

Molly walked into the house and tossed her bag on the couch. "Mom, I'm home," she called out. She heard the muted slam of the dryer door and her mom came into the kitchen from the laundry room.

"Hello, dear, school go all right today?" her mom asked.

"Yeah, everything was fine. No surprises."

"Well, that's good. Can you come help me fold clothes in my bedroom?

Molly shrugged her shoulders. "Sure, mom, I'll be right there." Her mom disappeared down the hall and Molly grabbed some chips and a diet soda, following her to where a large mound of clothes lay on her mother's king size bed. She placed the soda and chips on the nightstand next to the bed, then sat on the edge with her mom and picked up a pair of her slacks, folding them into a neat bundle and laying it beside her. While they folded clothes, the two chatted, almost like Molly and Janice did, but with a bit of a more serious tone. This continued until all the clothes lay folded and Molly had a pile to take to her room. Rising from the bed, Molly leaned over to kiss her mom on the cheek, quickly said "I love you," and then moved out of her mom's bedroom and down the hall to her own.

She talked with her friends on her old cell until her mom called to her that dinner was ready. Molly put her phone on the bed as her mom didn't allow phones at the dinner table. She appeared at the dinner table and Barry was there, already diving into whatever delicacy sat before him. "Man," he said. "This looks amazing. Thanks, honey. I'm starved." He piled potatoes and meat on his plate and dug in.

"Say, Molly, how was school today?" Barry directed his question at

Molly. At the sound of his voice, Molly had to fight to keep from freezing up. She wanted to yell and scream at him, and maybe even stab him with her dinner knife. But all she got out was a garbled, "Fine, nothing special."

"Ha! Just like me when I was her age. Nothing ever happens at school they want to talk about." At the lack of any input from Molly or her mom, Barry looked at the two of them, then lowered his head, said, "Okay, whatever, just thought I'd make some polite dinner conversation."

Molly looked up from her plate, her eyes going back and forth between her mother and Barry. There was a tension there, but Molly couldn't identify what it was. Did her mother know what Barry was doing to her? Did she know Molly was planning to run away the next morning? No, there's no way she could know that. What's going on between them?

"You two all right?" she asked. Barry looked a little guilty, and her mom bit her lower lip in suppressed anger. Wow! Something *was* going on.

Finally, her mother spoke. "No, dear, nothing's going on. Barry just got home a little later than I expected last night and he's going out again tonight, I guess. So it's just me, here for the rest of the night. Let's just eat our dinner."

They ate the rest of the meal, mostly in silence. After they were done, Molly and her mom cleaned up and washed the dishes while Barry headed to the living room and the TV, intending to head out later.

With the dishes clean and the kitchen in acceptable order, Molly excused herself to her room, where she supposedly watched streaming videos on her cell or texted her friends. She texted Jan and they locked down what Molly was going to do the following morning after first period.

She slept fitfully, waking with starts at the slightest noise. Finally, the room lit up as the sun slowly climbed above the horizon. At six am her alarm buzzed and Molly began her routine. She finished hurriedly, donning a pair of light slacks, a basic blouse, and her normal tennis shoes, anxious yet sad to begin this journey.

Eating something for breakfast totally revolted her. She was just too nervous. Molly grabbed her school backpack for probably the last time and headed out the front door onto the porch and stepped onto the sidewalk, making her way to the bus stop. There She and Janice talked some, but the conversation was subdued.

The bus picked them up and finished its route before pulling into the school and letting the students disembark. Soon after, a loudspeaker announced across the school grounds that first period would start in ten minutes. Molly made her way to class but sat the whole time, fidgeting. The period lasted only sixty minutes, but to Molly it seemed like forever. Finally, class was over and Molly made her way to a side door many kids knew about where they could slip out unnoticed, perhaps for a quick cigarette. She slipped out and walked to Janice's house. She approached the house from the opposite way she normally did and made for the garage. On the side away from the house, she found her duffel bag wrapped in a tarp, safe and dry. She unwrapped the bag from the tarp, double checked the contents, then slung the strap over her shoulder and walked to the sidewalk again, making her way to the bus stop for public transportation. It would be a fair walk and she wished she had a ride, but that was impossible, of course. She didn't want to leave any trail of her departing this area she used to call home.

Tickets cost more at the transit station than online and she only had enough money for Crescent City, not bigger cities like Sacramento or Los Angeles. Molly wasn't too upset about this. At least she would be out of Utah. She would see what developed after she got to California. Boarding the bus, she took a seat three quarters of the way at the rear. She decided it was a suitable spot. Too far forward and every time someone boarded or exited, she would be disturbed. Too far back, and the fumes from the bus exhaust seeping thru the fuselage would make her sick. The seat she selected was a suitable option. The bus soon pulled away from the curb, exiting the depot. Molly watched the buildings flow past her window, tears flowing down her face as she began her journey.

After a while, the bus traveled beyond the city and entered the highway, moving up to its normal cruising speed. The muted growl of the engine, initially loud, faded into background noise as Molly fell asleep, exhausted from the stress of the past twenty-four hours. The bus moved across the state, occasionally stopping to pick someone up or drop someone off.

Molly had packed some food for the journey, but she was glad when the bus made a rest stop where she could get off and grab a bite to eat and stretch her legs. Ordinarily, she would have a salad, but she was hungry and ordered a chicken burger with fries and a drink from the food counter. She sat on a stool at the counter when her new phone buzzed. Startled, Molly dug through her purse, found the phone. It was Janice, of course. She raised the phone to her ear. "Janice, what's going on?"

"Oh, hi. I just wanted to check in with you. Your mom's asking about you. Not too freaked out yet." Molly immediately felt a pang of guilt in her gut for what she was doing to her mother, but it was better this way.

"Well, you keep quiet. You don't know where I am," Molly frantically told her.

"I know, I know," said Janice. "And you're right, I really don't know where you are. You never told me where you were going."

"I didn't know myself until I got to the bus depot." Molly paused, listening closely, when the bus driver announced it was time to reboard. "Listen, I'll text you when I get to where I'm going. I can't talk anymore. The bus is leaving. I've got to go, bye." Molly hung up before Janice could delay her further. She placed her phone back in her bag as she got off the stool and quickly boarded the bus, settling into a semi-comfortable position for the continuing excursion. Molly was okay with the trip taking fifteen to sixteen hours, but after about five or six hours of monotonous travel, she was ready to get off the bus forever. It was getting on to be early evening, and her bus was due to arrive in California at about eight pm. Once there, she needed to find a place to stay and then get a job. She didn't have a place for tonight even, something she overlooked in making her plans. Oh well, she would find something. As she thought about her circumstances, Molly drifted back into a fitful slumber.

The sounds of the bus entering the city roused Molly from her rest, and she sat up to look out the window. They were still on the freeway, but the traffic noises bouncing off nearby buildings intensified the racket. Peering through the glass, she gazed at a couple of skyscrapers reaching for the sky, with hundreds of windows dotting the sides of the immense buildings. Until now, Molly had never been outside Utah. This new city was a completely new experience for her. At first, it was all so different and amazing it overwhelmed her senses, but as she viewed her surroundings further, she detected a level of dirt, grime, and neglect on a few of the buildings. She didn't expect that. In her mind, she envisioned a larger expanse of buildings and streets than her hometown, of course. But they were all clean, refuse free, with little need for repair. What lay before her was disappointing in its griminess. She hoped the rest of her new life would not be so tarnished. It brought a stark reality to what might be construed as a bleak beginning.

About twenty minutes later, the bus pulled into the station and passengers disembarked. Molly collected her hand and duffel bags from the overhead bins and made her way off the bus, exiting onto the sidewalk in front of the transit station doors. Hitching her duffel bag over one shoulder, she spotted a soda vending machine and worked her way through the throngs of people, at last standing in front of the machine, depositing the coins necessary to receive an ice cold soda delivered in an aluminum can. "Ahh," she said, her taste buds anticipating the first splash of a cold drink against the back of her throat. Her last meal must have had a lot of salt in it, because she felt overwhelmingly thirsty. She reached for the can, pulling back the metal ring tab and slammed the can against her mouth. She tried not to chug the drink like a truck driver or high school football player, but it was hard. After a few gulps, she slowed down and began savoring the effervescence of the soda, and the sweet taste of the drink itself. Wow, did that taste wonderful!

With drink in hand, she wandered past the ticket counters and luggage storage racks, venturing outside the station to the sidewalk. The blast of noise coming from the street was almost deafening for a young girl coming from a small town. She soon adjusted to the noise however and began walking down the boulevard, taking in the somewhat subdued sites before her eyes. Not too much to see in this area of town except buildings, factory fronts, taverns, and greasy spoons. Also, humanity in this neighborhood did not include many members of a higher clientele. Most were dirty, unkempt, drunk, or all three. Molly avoided them, rushing down the sidewalk as quickly as she could. Some men exhibited a curious interest in her and glanced at her body, but, in truth, they spent the vast majority of their energy in procuring their next fix, whatever that might be. Soon Molly was out of the area and left them behind.

One thing that surprised Molly about herself was her lack of fear in the situation she was in. She wasn't afraid. In fact, she was excited about getting away from Barry and starting her new life. She didn't want to hurt her mother; she loved her, but she just couldn't stay in that house with Barry one more night. Sometimes he pounced on her, pulling her to the sofa or her bedroom and satisfying himself quickly, leaving Molly in agony and humiliation. After he left, she would lie on her bed crying, eventually sitting up and pulling herself together. A shower afterwards was standard because she felt so dirty.

First things first, Molly said to herself. *It's late and I need a room, but I'm so hungry I need to eat first. But where?* She knew nothing about the streets of Crescent City. She picked Crescent City for no other reason than she could afford the trip and still have money left over. It may not be a super Megopolis like Los Angeles or Sacramento, but it had its charm. She felt good about traveling here.

But now, as she walked down the sidewalk, she couldn't feel more overwhelmed and vulnerable. Her definite plans upon arrival were falling apart, despite her confidence. How long would it take for her to find a place, a job, and right now, some food? She felt utterly lost. She continued to walk through the city, trudging block after block, falling into a deep depression. Tears fell down her cheeks as she contemplated what now seemed a bleak future. What had she done?

As she crossed a dark alley between two apartment buildings, without warning, an arm shot out, grabbed her by her upper arm, and yanked her into the alley. It happened in a split second. Nobody saw her disappear. Molly looked in terror at the face of the man who gripped her. He was barely taller than she was, about five foot four. Dirty and grimy, he smelled awful. "Stop!" Molly cried. "Let me go, you're hurting me!" The man tried to grab her purse, ignoring the duffel bag Molly carried in her other hand. That was his mistake. Molly swung the duffel bag with all her strength and the bag collided with the dirty man's head. It spun him around and he released her, falling to the ground.

"You little bitch! I'll teach you!" He climbed slowly to his feet, but Molly hadn't waited for him to get back up. She bolted from the alley and ran down the street, mindful of the other alleyways she passed, giving them a wide berth.

Finally, she stopped feeling sorry for herself and was determined to make the best of it. Looking up from the sidewalk, she found herself standing in front of a small Mexican restaurant. Aromas coming from the restaurant were heavenly. The shop front displayed a few lights, with the menu fastened to a large front window, facing out so passersby could read it and get an idea of what the restaurant offered. Through the window, she viewed a nice, clean place with some booths, but mostly tables and chairs. Toward the back, she recognized an older cash register, with a very pretty Hispanic woman behind the bar where the register sat, pouring beers from a small selection of taps. The woman wore a traditional Hispanic dress with flowing skirts and embroidery all around. She finished pouring the beer, took the tray, and walked towards three customers sitting at a small table. Placing the beers on the table, she looked up and saw Molly through the glass and smiled. Molly, after a second, shyly smiled back. The woman gestured for her to come in and Molly, now hungrier than ever, opened the door and came inside. The woman came over to her, the serving tray now held flat against her side.

"Hello, little one. You look pretty forlorn and lost. Did you know that? Come here, child, sit down over here and talk to me. I have a few minutes."

Molly accepted her invitation and sat at a table the woman indicated in the corner, out of the way. "Thank you, ma'am. I am really tired and scared."

"I can certainly see that, my dear. What has you in such a state?"

And with that question, Molly's reserve broke, and she poured out her troubles. She told this strange, beautiful woman about her mother's relationship with Barry, their financial struggles, and Barry's increasing sexual abuse towards her. As she spoke, the women's eyes softened even more as she listened, and then hardened to glints of black onyx when she heard about Barry. She contained her anger such that Molly didn't notice, but underneath she was seething fury. “So, you left because of this monster?” she asked Molly.Tears were brimming in her eyes as she spoke. Molly’s story finally ran down and she sat quietly, sipping some water the women had fetched while Molly unburdened herself. To the woman’s question, she nodded numbly as she remembered her past.

“And your mother does not know where you are. Si?” Molly nodded again. “Do you want me to call her to come get you?”

Molly thought for a second, then shook her head no. “That wouldn’t change anything. I’d go back to that house and, unless I said something, Barry would start molesting me again. And if I did say something, and Mom threw him out, our money problems would just get worse. And if I did say something and Mom did nothing about it, that would just break my heart and I would die.”

The woman was silent for a moment, then spoke. “Child, you are welcome to stay here, at least for tonight. There is a small room upstairs that used to belong to Jose, my son. He is off at college now and won’t be back for months. Please, let me take care of you and help ease your pain.” Molly looked at the woman, stared at her eyes and the compassion there, and nodded. “Yes, I would like to stay. Can I get something to eat?”

The woman laughed and rose from the table. “Of course! Maria! Burritos for this one! And a fresh glass of something to drink.” The woman turned to Molly. “My name is Juanita. What is your name?”

Molly replied softly, “Molly.” The energy in the room picked up again as Juanita stood up to make her way to a nearby table.

“Molly. What a beautiful name. Some people call me Mama. You are welcome to do so. I must go now. I have neglected my customers for too long. Enjoy yourself and relax. We will talk much more when my restaurant closes.” And with that, Juanita whisked away from the table in a flurry of brightly colored skirts, stopping at the next table to inquire the needs of the customers there. Molly felt better than she had for a long time.

Later that night, after the restaurant closed, Juanita took Molly to the little bedroom she mentioned earlier. The room was modest, yet well-maintained, and furnished with a double bed, dresser, and floor lamp. It also had its own bathroom and shower. A medicine chest, hanging on the wall above the sink, displayed a mirror. She was grateful for the space, though. Sleeping on the streets did not appeal to her. Although Juanita was obviously tired, she helped Molly put away her things and then said good night and left Molly to her thoughts. Molly undressed, hanging her clothes in the small closet. She felt dirty and grimy from the bus trip, and took a shower, then brushed her teeth and gave her hair a quick brush. Fatigue from lack of sleep and the stress of the day's events caught up with her and she collapsed on the bed, pulling the covers over her and fell asleep instantly.

A loud, metallic bang coming from the cantina-like restaurant below woke Molly up hours later. She rolled on her back and looked at the ceiling for a bit, then rose and padded on bare feet to the bathroom. After using the facilities, she pulled out a pair of jeans and a blouse out of her duffel bag, along with a clean bra, panties, and socks. All of this went together with her shoes and she headed downstairs to the lovely smell of Mexican food being prepared.

"Ahh, there is my lost little one!" exclaimed Juanita. "How are you feeling today? Sleep well?"

Molly smiled sheepishly, then looked down at the floor. "Yes, ma'am. I guess I slept pretty good."

"I know you must be hungry. We don't have much ready yet, but I will make you some bean and cheese burritos. They will restore you and fill you up. Sit down over there and I will get it for you." Molly sat where Juanita showed her and in minutes Juanita was back with a large plate brimming with several burritos. "Here at my restaurant, I make many burritos for my staff. We eat like family. Please, help yourself." Juanita left but quickly returned with chips and salsa, also a pitcher of water and ice, along with a glass for Molly to drink from. While Molly dug into the delicious food, Juanita sat with her, occasionally directing her employees to perform certain tasks. Everyone bustled about like a fine dance.

The cooks chopped meats and vegetables and put them into cooking pans in the kitchen. The team added heaping mounds of black and pinto beans into enormous pots of water and set the burners low to simmer them and make them savory. Behind the kitchen counter was the dishwasher station where plates, glasses and silverware were meticulously washed. Out in the main room, tables were set with fresh tablecloths and flowers. Juanita kept an eye on all of it. Nothing eluded her eye. Everyone seemed good natured and friendly. Two male staff gave Molly a friendly once-over until they saw Juanita frowning at them, then they quickly averted their gaze elsewhere and whisked off to finish getting ready for the lunch crowd, scheduled to appear in about an hour.

Even before they were open, a line of customers began forming at the door, some of them long time customers, eager to claim their favorite seats. When the restaurant finally opened, a crowd stood in front of the restaurant. Some chatted with each other, others were together as couples. It was interesting to see the group relaxed, friendly, smiling. It brought joy to Molly's heart, and she smiled too. The past twenty-four hours of feeling lost and alone started creeping back to its home of darkness.

After Molly ate her breakfast and watched people for a bit, she went back upstairs to the room Juanita let her use and sat on the bed, thinking about her next move. Staying here was certainly an option, but that was up to Juanita, not her. What would she do if Juanita asked her to move on? And what about a job? Her money was running out fast. The amount she had brought with her drained from her pocket at an alarming rate. At this rate, it wouldn't be long before she was completely broke. She could think of many more questions, and just thinking about them drained the energy from her body and soul. It was too soon for her to focus on that. She exhaled sharply, her bangs flipping away from her face, then returning. She decided to shelve everything for the moment and go down to see if Juanita could use her help.

Entering the restaurant from the back stairs, Molly saw that the lunch crowd had dwindled, with just a few patrons left. Maria, one of the servers, was taking an order at one table while Juanita worked the register. Two male cooks manned the grill, while a young man quickly washed dishes using an industrial machine. Molly had seen these machines before, and often wondered why they weren't used by the general public. Dishes went through and came out the other end, still a bit wet, but a towel would dry them off and make them ready to use again. Molly waited until Juanita finished handing her customer their change, walking up to her as they moved off. "Juanita, er- mama, is there anything I can do to help around here? You've been so nice to me. I'd like to help out somehow." Juanita smiled. She was always smiling. "Why, of course, I would like to talk to you about that. Come, sit over here with me."

Together, they moved to a nearby table and sat down. Juanita motioned to Maria for some water for the two of them. It came quickly. Juanita would not tolerate a slow waitress. "My dear, I'm glad to hear you say you would like to help. I would like that too. In fact, I wanted to ask if you were willing to help Maria with managing the tables. It can get to be too much for just one person and everyone else has their own jobs. I act as hostess and cashier. Maria waits on tables. Jose and Phillippe are my cooks, and Micah is my dishwasher. Another person to help Maria during peak hours would be God smiling on me from above. I can't pay you too much, but I offer you the room you are in now, plus meals and a small salary, if that would interest you. I could really use your help." Juanita was now very serious, her dark eyes gazing at Molly with repressed passion. It didn't take long for Molly to decide. Here she had a place to stay, food, and a paycheck, all in one sweep. She knew it wouldn't be too hard to learn the ins and outs of waitressing from Maria. It would be a place to start her journey in a new city.

"Yes, Mama. That would be nice. I would like to stay very much. Thank you."

Juanita grinned and stood. "This is good," she said. "I will introduce you to the staff and get you started with Maria, if that's alright. We have some groups coming this evening and your help would be most welcome." Molly stood with her. "Of course, Mama, I'd love to get started."

Chapter 28

Molly was a very affable girl, and she blended in quickly with the other staff members. Although she was not Hispanic, the others welcomed her and seemed eager to show her the business. Maria became like a big sister to her, showing Molly how to interact with customers, taking orders, providing drinks. How to carry trays piled with customer orders and not spill the drinks or the food. Molly thought it was all exciting and great fun. It was like the family she always wanted. Molly was an only child, the family cut short by her father's car accident.

By the time her mother married again, both Barry and she were older and didn't particularly desire children. For Molly, that had some perks, but in the long run, it wasn't hard for her to feel lonely. All her friends had brothers or sisters, often both. Molly frequently felt left out when conversations turned to family life and sibling interchanges. Now, she had a family too.

Weeks passed. It was a sultry night in August when everything changed for Molly. While Molly and Maria had become fast friends, tonight was a family event Maria had to attend, so Molly was left to entertain herself. Instead of hanging around the restaurant or reading upstairs, she decided to use her time to get familiar with her new city. She dressed in a light cotton dress, socks, and sneakers to stay comfortable while exploring the neighborhood. With the money left in her purse, combined with what Juanita paid her, Molly wanted to look for a clothing store where she might find a blouse or pair of shoes she might like. The clothing stores where she lived were small, mom and pop stores, without a lot of selection.

She couldn't find much nearby. When Maria returned, she planned to convince her to go to one of the few malls in the city later in the week.

Molly found a blouse she liked while window shopping, despite thinking there wasn't much clothing selection in the area. She wanted to relax some before heading back to the restaurant. Although it was her night off, she relished working alongside her new companions. Besides, there wasn't much else to do. Her room had no TV, and she didn't want to use up the data on her new phone. If she worked, she got paid, or at least fed, which, at this point in her life, was ok.

She cut through a deserted mini-mall on her way to Juanita's restaurant, intending to grab a snack at a small shop near the restaurant. Immersed with her thoughts, she didn't notice the man coming up behind her from between two buildings until he violently grabbed her and threw her against the wall of one building, stunning her and knocking her cell phone out of her hand. While dazed, he half carried her to a gray, 2002 Dodge Neon sedan, waiting close by at the curb. Then he shoved her into the back seat. He quickly put duct tape across her mouth and wrapped more tape around her legs and, pulling her arms behind her, wrapped those with tape too. Molly recovered and began moving around and screaming, which unnerved him, even though he knew no one could hear her. He punched her in the face and she fell back against the seat cushion, totally disoriented and dazed. Before she could help herself, she passed out. The unknown attacker got into the driver's seat and drove away from the curb without attracting attention. He stayed within the speed limit, driving through town to the outskirts where some of the older residential track houses and pulled into the garage of an older home, effectively disappearing from sight. Next, he wrestled the now unconscious Molly out of the backseat and half carried, half dragged her into the house, his hands occasionally fondling her as he struggled to keep a handhold on her and not drop her to the floor. Man, he really struck gold this time. This girl was super hot. He ached with just the thought of what he would do to her later. But first things first. He had to get things set up.

Finally, her abductor managed to get her into the specially prepared master bedroom next to his and rolled her onto the bed. The windows had thick drapes over them, but truth be told, he had also nailed three-quarter inch plywood panels across the windows. He then painted them white to look like regular drapes, so that the total effect from the outside looked like a quaint little home for a small family or someone just starting out. Inside the room, however, between all the studs, ceiling joists and subflooring, he had stuffed insulation and then double sheetrock.

On top of all that, he stapled egg cartons on all four walls, the ceiling, the floor except for a walkway, and the door. He was confident that no one could hear anything coming from that room, unless they were in the house, and maybe not even then. He then handcuffed Molly to the bed with police professional double lock steel handcuffs he purchased online, one for each wrist, and one for each leg. Couldn't have her escaping now, could we? He left the duct tape over her mouth after making sure she could breathe through her nose properly. He once read a book where someone died because, while restrained, the victim gagged with duct tape over their mouth and suffocated. The abductor who tied him up didn't notice the victim had a cold or allergies or something. They suffocated when the guy went off to do something and didn't come back for several hours.

He was all set now. The girl was still knocked out, and he wanted a conscious participant in the upcoming activities, so he left her handcuffed to the bed and went into the kitchen to make himself something to eat. He smiled to himself, thinking he was going to need his energy later.

Chapter 29

The medical examiner and his team uncovered five children in the backyard of John Fields' house and suspected that more might be buried elsewhere on the property. The medical examiner and his team somberly processed the recovered bodies throughout the long night under the large tent covering the crime scene. Police personnel involved here treated the taped off area with a reverence and dignified respect for the tragically compact forms that took up a frightfully small fraction of the table set up for the coroner's use. The tiny figures accentuated the table, making it look even larger.

More than one outwardly tough looking police officer appeared to be fighting back tears or even openly crying as they brought the bodies to the medical examiner's table.

CSI personnel marked and photographed evidence in the house before collecting and bagging it. They focused on the basement room and removed stained fabric, hairs, flesh, and blood from the mattress and handcuffs. Left on a bureau were recordable DVD's, recklessly stacked next to a small camera on a tripod with the lens pointed towards the mattress.

On the DVD's, names were inscribed with a black felt pen. The conclusion was obvious. Sargent Jack Stromberg stood in the living room, talking and answering questions of various staff, one hand on his hip while the other accentuated his words. Most of the personnel were dressed in cleanroom appearing outfits, wearing gloves, booties and hair coverings so as not to contaminate the area. Lieutenant Anderson stood in the kitchen, which was already processed, so he wasn't garbed like the others but wore a suit jacket over a pair of Docker slacks. His Oxford shoes, gleaming at the beginning of the day, now looked repressed, dull, covered in a layer of dust from the house, and spotted with dirt from the yard. As he finished a conversation with Mace, Jack, dressed much as Anderson was in a dark gray suit jacket and slacks, walked up to him.

"Hey, Lieutenant, word is out. Press is showing up." Anderson looked out to the street and saw a TV van pull into position while a camera crew climbed out of a Ford Expedition. A journalist Anderson recognized from one of the local TV stations headed their way.

"Damn, how do they find out so fast?" Anderson turned to Stromberg. "Do we have a leak in our department?" he asked.

"Don't know, sir," said Jack. "These things just get out." After looking at the TV journalist heading towards them, he turned back to the Lieutenant. "You going to say something to them?" Anderson shook his head.

"It's too soon. Hell, we don't know yet if we found all the bodies just in the trees, let alone the rest of the property. It's too bad our vigilante killed this guy because now we'll never know if we found all of them. Keep them back behind the tape. I'll make a statement after talking with the chief." With that, Anderson moved into a group of officers and began directing activities. Stromberg, tasked with keeping the press back, made his way to Mariana Cortez, the journalist Anderson had dodged the interview with.

"Hi, Mariana, the Lieutenant isn't ready to make a statement yet so you need to keep back behind the tape." He politely held his hand out, palm upraised, indicating she should stop and turn around. Mariana looked over his shoulder to see Lieutenant Anderson engaged with other officers. She exhaled loudly, clearly frustrated, knowing she had no choice but to comply. Mariana motioned to her cameraman, who already had a Sony MC2500 camera on his shoulder, ready to shoot. Mariana faced the camera and, at a nod from her, he pressed record and a little red light above the camera lens lit up and Mariana began reporting about the crime scene.

"We are here on the outskirts of Bandon at the intersection of 187th and Farmcrest, where it appears an alleged homicide has taken place.

Tragically, the homicide may be a young child, and there might be more than one. The lead officer on this case, Lieutenant James Anderson, is still gathering information on the crime scene and is unable to speak with us." At this point, Jack saw the trap but was too slow in attempting to get out of range of the camera or the news journalist. "However, I just spoke with Sargent Jack Stromberg, the lieutenant's second in command. Sargent, what can you tell us about what's happening here?"

Jack cursed himself for being too slow and not getting away from the media quick enough, but he shrugged his shoulders and allowed Mariana to get close enough to put a microphone in his face.

"Mariana, at approximately eleven am this morning, Bandon police received an anonymous tip regarding a possible homicide at this location. Officers arrived at the scene within ten minutes of being notified and began processing the area, setting up crime scene tape, isolating the area, etcetera. Preliminary results show a potential crime has been committed here, but, as you said, we are still gathering data, and it will take some time to gather all the evidence within the cordoned off area." Jack turned to go, but Marianna was too quick for him.

"It's been said that children may be involved. Can you speak to that?" she asked. Jack looked at her, and she could see the hurt in his eyes. But all he said was "I'm sorry, I can't comment on that until we know more. The Lieutenant will try to issue a statement later today, possibly tomorrow morning." Before Marianna could ask another question, Jack turned and walked away from the camera.

Damn, thought Marianna, *it must be really bad. Jack has never walked away from me like that before.*

Although Marianna scooped the other stations, it wasn't long before more news correspondents arrived in television vans, SUV's and sedans. Helicopters arrived, hovering over the area, recording everything, looking to get a better shot or an unexpected detail to add to the story. Anderson was grateful he had ordered raising the tents first thing. It kept prying eyes from getting too much information before they were ready to release it. Much of what they said on TV would be assumptions, so it was marginally better to have a press conference and release some information to keep panic and fear at a minimum. What Anderson had to say to the press so far wouldn't help much in that regard, as the victims in this horrible crime were children, all under the age of twelve. He imagined a reduction in the number of kids walking to school in the next few days. More kids will use buses or their parents will drive them. And yes, some concerned parents would keep their children home, possibly until the killer was caught.

CHAPTER 30

Interstate 5 is a pretty interesting road with all kinds of scenery bedecking either side as you travel down its path. My eyes scanned side to side, taking in the trees, the grass, an occasional house sitting next to the road, and checking my dashboard regularly, making sure all was well with my rig.

The drive from Bandon to Reno, Nevada, took approximately twelve hours, with breaks and meals included. I considered going to California and just stay on the Interstate, but California cities didn't give me warm and fuzzies as they were pretty urban and a sprawling metropolis of people, noise, and pollution. Plus, their laws and regulations were more rigorous, and I wanted to disappear and not show up on someone's radar. Nevada was a little more relaxed, plus I had worked at this RV park before. Some businesses along the coast allowed RV's and trailers to camp overnight in the parking lot, Walmart being one of them. If all else failed, I figured I could try that route, which was something new for me. Grace and I preferred a more arranged environment, with hookups, bathrooms, trees and grass, with the smell of a wood fire wafting in the breeze. Spending the night in a Walmart parking lot was not the ideal set up for me. I was making good time and felt confident that I would find a place to stay the night before continuing on to Nevada.

CHAPTER 31

Molly lay in the darkness, her mind swirling round and round. She remembered walking through the deserted shopping mall and the man jumping from the shadows and grabbing her, slamming her against the wall of the building, knocking the wind out of her. Weak and disoriented, she felt herself dragged to a nearby vehicle and tossed inside. When she started struggling and tried to scream, he punched her and she passed out. She couldn't remember anything until now when she woke up. Still dazed, she felt restraints holding her arms and legs on what felt like a bed mattress, which wasn't good.

Molly feared the worst. Barry, her stepfather, had introduced her, however reluctantly, to sex when she was fifteen. It was the reason she fled the home she grew up in after a few months of it and couldn't stand it any longer. And now this. It wouldn't be too long before the monster she now faced came back in and molested her. And maybe did other things to her as well. She needed to be strong and wait for a chance to escape. She tried yelling when she first woke up, but she could tell by the dull and flat timbre of her voice that the room was soundproofed. Any chance of a rescue would have to come from her. No knight in shining armor was coming. It was up to her. She would watch. And wait for her chance. And then she would escape any way she could.

CHAPTER 32

I made it to Joe Creek Waterfalls RV resort before I called it quits and pulled up to the ranger hut and paid for a spot with electricity, figuring to use the facilities and potable water on board rather than hook everything up since I only planned to spend the night. It was late, so I pulled into my spot, then plugged in the electrics. After that I went to the restrooms and did my business, then came back.

As dinner cooked, I raised my antenna dish, intending to listen to the news. It made no mention of the activity in Bandon on the local or national news, which pleased me. I figured no news was good news, so I ate my dinner, washed the dishes, took my pills and watched some TV for a bit. It had been a long drive, though, so it wasn't long before my head began bobbing and I crawled into bed and fell into a deep sleep.

The sounds of other people rising to go fishing or making breakfast interrupted my dream slumber, and I eventually came awake. The sounds of families heightened the pleasure of lying there listening to conversations, campfires crackling, and occasional dogs barking. It helped me to forget my cancer and the horrors I uncovered the day before. Eventually I crawled out of bed, showered, shaved, fixed breakfast and got back on the road. Once again, the day shone clear, with no signs of rain. With any luck, I would reach my desired state park and set up camp. Negotiating a stay with the park hosts in exchange for park work remained a possibility. Depending on who it was, they were quite relaxed in that regard.

My drive was uneventful. I stopped for gas once along the way and pulled into the park just about four o'clock. My instincts were correct, and I was able to finagle a space in exchange for a stint working there. After setting up, I wandered around the park a bit to get the lay of the land, although I had been here a few times before and the layout was familiar to me. Nonetheless, I had developed this habit over the years and it had become somewhat of a ritual. Until she passed, Grace and I took this walk together, especially the first night we arrived and often after dinner. It was just something that felt right doing.

Afterwards, I made dinner and watched the news. There must be a clamp on the Bandon story because there was still no information. Well, that wouldn't last much longer, I was sure, and then all hell would break loose and it would quickly become the lead story, at least for a couple of days. Anyway, I was out of it for now. I wanted to lie low for a bit, take stock of what I was doing. I could already feel the urge to Google the sex offenders' websites in this area and make new plans. There was no way this would have a happy ending. I was a dead man any way I looked at it.

CHAPTER 33

Bandon, a relatively small town, only had one vehicle for transporting dead bodies to the morgue. The coroner's office and Anderson's team worked together to carefully tag and organize the bodies and related evidence found both inside and around the pit. This was going to be a major job putting all this together and Sheryl Michaels, the medical examiner, had requested help from other cities to assist. The story was bound to break loose now, Anderson thought. No getting around it.

Anderson and Stromberg rode together back to the station. Anderson went into his office to prepare for his meeting with the mayor and chief of police to bring them up to speed. Stromberg first visited the coffee machine and then deposited himself at his desk to begin the immense job of filling out the paperwork for each victim. He could get the papers started, but the coroner would have to help with providing some leads so he could begin identifying the bodies. This promised to be a logistical nightmare. Jack assumed this event would get priority over anything else in Sheryl's department. But it would still take time to organize the bodies, check for identifying marks or paperwork found on the bodies. Maybe a photo ID or some schoolwork, perhaps. Autopsies would be performed on most of the kids. They would have to check evidence found in the house against the bodies. Sheryl might take snapshots of the heads of the children and attempt to cross reference them to a missing children's database. Cataloging the DVDs was a daunting task. A big help was the name of a person on the DVD. That helped tremendously.

CHAPTER 34

Lieutenant Anderson called ahead while he and Stromberg were in transit from the crime scene. Both the mayor and the Chief were waiting in the Chief's office for his report. Anderson used the gender-neutral bathroom to freshen up before heading to the Chief's office on the floor above his office. The stairs were about the only exercise he got most days, although he tried to get to the gym when he could. Besides, the building was only three stories high. It wasn't a superhuman effort by any means.

He reached the top of the stairs, stopping for a moment to catch his breath. Man! He really needed to get to the gym more often! After a minute, he collected himself, moving down the hall to the chief's office. Approaching the door, his eyes fell on the name, Jason Brock, Chief of Police, etched in the glass window encased in the center of the upper half of the door. Lieutenant Anderson was perfectly happy in his role as police captain and did not envy or desire the job of chief of police. He had no wish to become mired down in the political swampland that was Brock's environment and was completely happy to chase down the bad guys and put them behind bars. It made for a slightly subservient role on his part, but he was okay with that.

As he opened the door, the mayor and Brock ended their conversation, whatever it was, and turned to look at him. Anderson didn't know the mayor as well as he did the chief of police. They didn't move in the same circles. It was only in times like these they even spoke to one another. Anderson turned and closed the door behind him. Brock motioned for him to take a seat in front of his desk.

"Chief, mayor," began the lieutenant. "It's been a hell of a day."

Brock's eyebrows raised a trifle as he took in this statement. The mayor's face was a display of raw, terrified emotion. Everyone in the room knew the basics of what they had discovered. It was Anderson's job to fill in the details, and they weren't going to be pleasant. "Why don't you tell us about it, Lieutenant," said Brock.

Despite his tough exterior, the lieutenant struggled to start the story. He reached into his vest pocket and pulled out his notebook, obviously intending to use it to help him keep his facts straight. After thumbing through a couple of pages and clearing his throat, he began reading from his notes.

"Last night at approximately four thirty pm, the station received a call from an unknown person. This person informed us he had just killed Johnny Fields, a convicted child molester and rapist. The caller also indicated there was more than one child's body on the premises, buried in the backyard near some trees. After giving us the address, he hung up." The mayor looked as though he would ask a question, but Brock raised a cautionary hand and suggested they wait until Lieutenant Anderson finished his narrative.

Anderson continued. "I immediately order two units to the address, and Stromberg and I headed there as well. Upon arrival, we entered the house and found Fields tied to a kitchen chair, shot through the head. He was shot in the legs as well. After confirming Fields was indeed deceased, we made our way to the backyard. At the back of the yard, under some freshly turned earth, we found the body of a young girl, approximately seven years old. My team immediately sealed off the area, and I contacted forensics and the medical examiner." Here Anderson stopped to collect himself. His next words displayed the tension he struggled to keep under control. "At the current time, we have uncovered five bodies in various stages of decomposition. There is a mixture of boys and girls, as in keeping with Johnny Fields' predilection from previous child molestation convictions." Here Anderson stopped. Brock began the debriefing from his side now.

"Do we know if there are any more bodies?" After his narration,

Lieutenant Anderson felt the tremendous pressure and horror of what he had just related to his superior. He had a glassy, faraway look in his eyes as he recalled seeing the bodies, one after the other, removed from the earth. Brock had to repeat himself to get Anderson's attention. "Lieutenant?" Anderson came back in to focus.

"Sorry, sir. We haven't finished scanning the entire grounds yet, so it's possible there might be more. One piece of information, while gruesome, might be of help." Brock stared at Anderson.

"And what information is that?" he asked. Anderson got a pained look on his face before he replied.

"A camera was setup and DVDs found in a room in the basement where Johnny kept his victims while abusing them. It's possible the DVD's can give us a head count and maybe determine how many victims there really are, but I don't envy the officer who gets assigned to watch these DVD's to determine the possible final number. And it's not foolproof, sir, as the movies may not include everybody. It's possible he worked his way up to his current activities."

Brock looked at Anderson, and then at the mayor. "No, I don't envy that person either," he said. "Do we have a lead on the person who called it in?" Anderson adjusted his seat before replying.

"Not really, sir. This gets a little involved. A couple weeks ago, an unidentified caller contacted us, informing us of another child molester violating his parole and working at an elementary school. We didn't pay it much attention because, as you know, we get these kinds of calls all the time. Plus, we were short staffed that week and unable to respond in a timely manner. Then this molester, Michael Bateman, kidnapped a young boy, raped him and killed him, leaving the boy's body in a dumpster. When it came out on the news, we received another call where my ass was chewed out by this same person for not listening to him and this young boy's blood was on my hands. Then this last call. We believe it's from the same person. His first call was from a pay phone we've determined was on Twelfth Street. His next call was using burner phones, so it's virtually impossible to track him down now."

"Do we have any leads at all on who this guy is?"

"Well, sir, we are checking cameras in the area, intending to follow Fields and see if we can find anybody following him, too. But the only real lead we have so far is this guys original call from that payphone, but if I were him, I would have made that call from a place far removed from where I lived or where I was operating, if that's what he's doing." Here, the mayor finally jumped in with a question of his own.

"What do you mean by that?"

"Sir, I think this guy may be a child molester vigilante, targeting them somehow, then hunting them down and killing them?" The mayor looked incredulous. "You really think that?"

"I don't know yet, sir. It's too soon to tell. We're still working on it."

Brock leaned back in his chair. "Ok, Jim, stay on it. Put as many resources as you can on solving this. We need to resolve this as soon as possible." Anderson started to say something, but Brock cut him off. "I know. The press already got wind of this. Mariana called me just before this meeting. Give her enough to keep her happy, but don't start a panic. We've got problems with this case already. If a child molester is exposed, that will excite the public, especially anyone with children. We may also have a vigilante who's going around murdering these molesters like some terminator. His actions could easily garner support and approval from Joe Public, and may even initiate copycats, and then all hell will break loose. Stay on this, Jim. It's dynamite." With that, Brock stood, and the lieutenant knew he was dismissed.

Back at his desk, Anderson let out a large breath of air as he sagged into his seat. "Son of a bitch," he muttered to himself. Gradually the sweats eased up, and his feeling of despair lifted, if only to a moderate degree. "We've got to get this guy," he muttered to himself. "And fast."

He leaned back in his chair, the unoiled springs creaking in protest. Staring at his monitor, Anderson crossed his arms and sat there, lost in thought, working out how to proceed with this case. The basics were obvious. A male suspect, description unknown, contacts the police department on more than one occasion to offer information to the police regarding one or more child molesters engaged in activities that violated their parole, or were illegal altogether. The police fail to respond in a timely manner.

We really need to get better at that, he thought to himself. Then a child dies, and the suspect calls again to berate the police for failing in their duties to respond to the information he gave them. Now, out of the blue, he calls yet again to tell them he's just murdered a known molester and several children are buried on this property out at the edge of town. The police respond and sure enough, there's a dead guy in the kitchen, blood everywhere, and a torture room downstairs in the basement, complete with a mattress, bondage material and recording equipment. Following up on the rest of the vigilante's information, they check the backyard and bingo, he's right again and we find multiple bodies buried in the dirt.

Some parts of what this guy is doing appear amateurish, unplanned, or at least not thought out completely. Other actions, such as using burner phones to disguise his identity, appear somewhat sophisticated. Huh, maybe this guy was a total amateur and the smart moves are what he saw on NCIS or in a movie. That actually makes a little sense. He'd have to throw it out to the department and determine the plausibility of the idea. Which meant he had to pull a meeting together as soon as possible. *Should he wait for the coroner's results or move forward with what he had so far?*

Personally, he had to admit; he agreed with the vigilante. Anderson also believed that these perverts were complete scum and society should remove them in any way possible. Some escaped incarceration entirely due to slick lawyers or technical mistakes on the part of various departments. Or, they were in control of their urges long enough to serve their sentences, get released, move to a new place, and start over. Statistics showed that between 14 and 26 percent of sex offenders repeat their crimes. Studies in Germany inferred sexual predators could respond to treatment, and should have the ability and the right to do so. Anderson wasn't so sure. He wondered if the predators just played the doctors in order to get the sympathy vote. Anderson firmly believed that most of them never responded to the treatment. Many of them continued with their passion, causing more pain and anguish for those unfortunate to be caught in their web.

But how to stop them? How to remove the urges of these troubled people and control the violence? Many thought castration should be the punishment for these kinds of crimes against children. Indeed, a study he read years ago stated that after castration, repeat offenders only acted point two percent of the time. Certainly, execution should be an option, some said. But in this civilized world of today, many also thought that wasn't who we are. That imprisonment, away from society, was the civilized way to deter these kinds of people. Anderson wasn't sure he agreed, but it wasn't his call to make. His job was to arrest violators of the law and right now, this molester vigilante needed to be found and brought in.

With that, he worked with Stromberg in setting up the meeting for tomorrow.

Chapter 35

Jennifer Carter was an adorable, eight-year-old girl with beautiful, long, dark hair her mother enjoyed brushing every night before bed. She lived in a little two-story house on the outskirts of Reno, Nevada, with her mom and dad. Her father was an engineer at a neighboring contract manufacturing firm, and her mother had just started back to work, now that Jenny was full time in school. Her mother took time off to have the baby and stayed home until Jenny entered first grade. With Jenny now suitably engaged in her education, she re-entered the workforce at another high-tech facility, similar to her husbands. She contemplated working in a casino, but turned it down, as it wasn't the kind of lifestyle she wanted to promote for her family. Also, she didn't quite trust herself around the gambling tables, and felt it was better to leave temptation alone. Besides, she enjoyed her work, her coworkers, the shift, plus it left her with plenty of time for her family.

Franklin sat in his van, watching Jenny play. Yesterday, Franklin was driving the company van when he spotted the little cutie and was immediately enraptured with her. After carefully following her home from school the day before, he returned to her street the next day, parking down the street. Jennifer's family lived in a suburban neighborhood. And, while plenty of houses surrounded the Carter property, most of them were empty during the day, as most owners or renters worked. It was an early release day for the school, and Jenny was home early, playing in the backyard. Jenny's parents were both still at work, but one of the neighborhood high school girls offered to watch Jenny until the shift ended for either parent and they could come home. Susan was a typical teenage girl, obsessed with boys, always on her cell, texting her girlfriends about who knows what, and generally giving little notice to young Jenny playing in the backyard. The backyard was fenced all the way around, except for a little gate. And that had a lock on it. What could go wrong?

Franklin was doing this on the fly, with little planning. But his need was so urgent he couldn't wait. And young Jenny was just so cute and adorable. He knew that today was an early release day, and he could see the teenage babysitter Susan in the front room texting her friends, essentially ignoring Jenny for the most part. If he was quick, he could snatch Jenny and be gone before Susan could react, if indeed she noticed anything. He decided to go for it, and started his van, easing forward until he came to the curb near the backyard fence. Jenny's back was to him, so she didn't see or hear him. The fence was a low, four-foot barricade offering little defense to a determined person. Franklin unlocked the passenger side of the van, then stepped out. In a fluid movement, he ran toward the fence. Placing both hands on the top railing, he vaulted over and was in the backyard. Before Jenny could turn around, he grabbed her and was heading back toward the fence. Jenny was such a small girl he vaulted back over the fence using one hand. In an instant, he was at his van, Jenny beginning to struggle against him, but not screaming yet. He opened the door, shoving her into the passenger seat, locked the door and ran around to the driver's side, sliding in to the seat in a smooth movement. The keys were in the ignition, and he had left the engine running. In seconds, he placed the van in drive and raced away from the curb.

Unfortunately for Jenny, Susan was so intent on texting, she didn't realize the little girl was gone for several minutes. By then, Franklin's vehicle was nowhere to be found.

Chapter 36

Molly lay on the bed, helpless. She tried her bonds several times, but there was no yielding in their steel embrace. She kept chiding herself for not being more careful, but she dropped her guard, forgetting she wasn't in her hometown anymore. Now, quite possibly, she could perish in this desolate place where no one would ever discover her. She could move her head a bit and take in the room where she was lying shackled. Incongruously, it stood decorated stylishly as a young girl's room, with a chest of drawers, a duvet across the bottom of the bed, and a closet.

A bedroom light hung from the ceiling in the center of the room. Some stuffed animals lay jumbled about on the bedroom floor. She would have liked this room, except for the ominous jangle of the handcuffs holding her to the bed. And the tangle of stuffed animals was out of place and gave her a cold, ominous feeling.

She heard a faint noise coming from the other side of the bedroom door. A clatter of dishes, then footsteps. Now muted for the moment, but then she heard water running and assumed it was the kitchen sink. It too shut off after a moment, and the footsteps moved her way.

Keys sounded outside the door, then the doorknob turned and Molly's abductor stepped into the room. He was a pudgy, flabby man, somewhat young, with short brown hair, about six feet tall, and seemed to have a calm smile. Dressed in jeans and a colored t-shirt, with laced up tennis shoes. He smiled at her now.

"Hi, I'm glad you're awake. You feeling ok?" were his first words to her.

Molly started thinking, *what the fuck? What's wrong with this guy?*

I'm lying here handcuffed by my hands and legs to a bed, duct tape over my mouth, kidnapped, and this creature wants to know if I'm ok? She made noises and gestures to him, showing she wanted him to remove the tape. He leaned over her, grabbed one end of the tape and pulled sharply. Molly groaned as the removal of the tape stung. Then she spoke, enraged.

"No, you dumb fuck, I'm not ok. I am chained to a bed against my will. My mouth has been taped shut for hours, and I really need a bathroom. Please take me to a bathroom right now." She glared at him with defiance and a complete rage. He stood there, staring at her, his smile gone. An odd look was on his face, and he reached out and slapped her sharply across her cheek. Molly was hit hard and tried to scream, but he was quick to cover her mouth again and all that came out was a little squeak. He then slugged her in the stomach, knocking the breath out of her. She lay there groaning as he sat on the edge of the bed and leaned into her face.

"Now," he said softly, menacingly, "I'm going to take you to the bathroom where you can do your business." He reached behind him and pulled out a long, fixed blade knife. He placed the blade against his forearm and shaved hairs off and they drifted to the floor. "See how sharp this knife is? I can shave with it. You behave yourself when I take you down the hall or I will mess you up so bad even your own mother won't recognize you. Am I clear?"

At the sight of the knife, Molly went all silent and her eyes got huge. She began to realize even more what a horrible, alarming position she was in. She shrank back from the knife, nodding her head up and done in little arcs very quickly. He sat there, looking at her with that blank face, and Molly felt truly, truly terrified.

"Good, I'm glad we understand each other. I'm going to release you. Don't try to run. All the doors are locked, and I boarded the windows over. There's no way out of this house unless I let you out. Understand?" Molly nodded vigorously again, and he unlocked the cuffs on her hands and legs, but then he cuffed her hands to each other, which would hamper any attempts at escape. She sat up and he helped her to her feet. He led her out the bedroom door and down the hall to the bathroom. As she stepped in, she turned to close the door, but he put his hand out. "No,

I don't think so," He said. "Leave the door open." Molly nodded glumly and moved to the toilet, expecting him to watch her pull her panties down and look at her while she used the toilet. He did neither. Even though the door was open and he could watch her if he wanted, instead he positioned himself a few feet down the hall, giving her a minor sense of privacy. The bathroom wasn't very large, but it had a counter with a sink and faucet, a shower bathtub combination, a ceiling fan, a mirror, and a window. The window was just as he described, boarded over with thick plywood. She turned on the fan, trying to hide her embarrassment.

He didn't rush her, and she took her time. When finished, she flushed the toilet and washed her hands. Exiting the bathroom, he walked behind her back to the bedroom, knife in hand, and told her to lie down. After he fastened her cuffs back to the bed, he reached under her dress and pulled down her panties, then cut them off with his very sharp knife, throwing the panties to the floor. Standing over her, he began removing his clothes, starting with his shirt. It wasn't long before he stood before her, naked and aroused. He moved onto the bed, positioning himself between her legs. When he was done, he picked up his clothes and stalked out, closing the door behind him. Soon after, she heard the shower running. She lay there where he had left her, spent, feeling dirty and even more humiliated and ashamed.

Chapter 37

I was only at the state park a couple of nights when the news came on the TV. Another child, a girl this time, had been taken right out of her own backyard in an area not too far from where I was now. The police were still collecting evidence, and they taped the crime scene off, but I went anyway, just to see what was going on. Several police cars sat parked at the Carter residence, along with two TV camera crews. Information was scant. It had happened so quickly. The young girl in the backyard, lost in playing with her toys, the babysitter on a couch in the living room, texting her friends. Not the smartest move when caring for another person's child, in my opinion.

They hired you to watch the kid, so watch the damn kid. Mom and dad were naturally distraught, hoping for a phone call that could bring news of their daughter's survival. I knew I wouldn't get much information here, but I wanted to see where it had happened. This was the first time I was in a place where possibly I could help. What I could do, that the local police couldn't, remained to be seen. Perhaps nothing, but my investigating the site galvanized me into action, and I knew I needed to get back in the game. There was no stopping me now.

I left the area, returning to my trailer and parked in front of it, clambering inside. Sitting at the dinette table, I flipped open my laptop and then logged in to find a local database of criminals. The database came up, and it astounded me at how many sexual predators were on file in Reno. And that was just the ones the police knew about. What about those we didn't know about, hiding in the background, lying low, careful to avoid detection? What about them?

I sorted through the records, searching for child predators near me. Some addresses were only a few miles from me, and I zeroed in on potential candidates to have their ticket punched. Although I made lists of all the people in these records, I applied some logic to my categories. Those that appeared to have served their sentences and weren't under arrest, I put in one category.

Those individuals who were currently serving time or waiting trial, I put in another. But the one category I focused most on was the bastards who were clearly guilty, but got off on some technicality and were loose on the streets. Or I felt the judge was way too lenient with them. Those creatures I examined more closely and in depth. I tried to find out as much as I could without making waves, being careful with my searches to not drill down too far. If something then happened to one of these scum and the police began a search through the IT department, I didn't know if they could find me. It was another reason to keep moving.

I intended to go back to my modus operandi of making my executions appear as accidents, even though I knew my slip up with Johnny Fields was on the police radar screen. If I was the only person doing this, eventually my activities would be uncovered. I wanted to think others felt as I and were doing their part to make this world a better place. But I wasn't sure, and I didn't know how to be sure.

Finally, I had my list of five creeps. I got into my truck and drove to the nearest address. It took about forty-five minutes with traffic, but that gave me time to look about and learn more about where I intended to operate. One thing I noticed right away, which should have occurred to me sooner, was how busy it was in the area of my first address. It would be prudent to patrol the area for a few days to determine any patterns. Another potential obstacle was cameras. They were everywhere. I would have to determine how to operate within the parameters of the camera's field of view, or focus my activities further out beyond the city limits where cameras weren't so prevalent. This first jaunt into unfamiliar territory required further contemplation. I didn't really want to limit myself to outlying areas. That seemed like a copout. On the other hand, with surveillance cameras everywhere, it would be even more important to make each execution seem like an accident so the police wouldn't review camera footage and find my truck everywhere.

I tried another three addresses and found the same scenario as the first. If the creep lived in the city limits, then the cameras protected him as much as anybody else. Damn. I needed to think about this. Perhaps coming to Reno had been a mistake. I stopped by a burger joint and grabbed a fast meal, driving back to my trailer as I ate with a heavy heart. Shit.

Back at the trailer, I grabbed a bottle of water and sat in my favorite chair. Leaning back, I took a long swig, savoring the taste of the ice cold water in my mouth and down my throat. Years ago, Grace and I got caught up in the craze of drinking bottled water. We were buying flats and flats of water bottles and becoming buried in plastic. Finally, we came to our senses and decided if we were going to drink bottled water we should drink the purest, and that's when we decided to drink distilled water in one gallon jugs. Distilled water sold for the same price as any other bottled water, and Grace thought it was the purest, so that's what we began doing.

After a while, it seemed second nature to buy distilled water whenever I needed fresh water. I once considered going back to tap water, but the taste was awful compared to what I habitually drank. Sure, I could have gone back to tap water or added a filter, but I figured what the hell, it was only me now anyway, and I really did like the taste of cold, distilled water.

Now that I was home among familiar things, I could think more clearly. With my head against the back of the chair, and my legs propped up on the ottoman, I let my mind drift in an effort to organize my thoughts and decide on what I would do next. Part of that was easy. Doing what I was doing made me happy, made me feel like I was making a difference. My cancer was in remission, which was terrific, but I knew it would come back some day. I wanted to rededicate myself to making these executions look like accidents. I couldn't have another Johnny Fields episode. It might already be too late in that regard.

I had to admit, putting a bullet through Johnny's head felt great, but was a mistake. I still wasn't clear in my mind why I called the police. Maybe I couldn't bear to think of those poor kids buried in the dirt for any longer than was necessary. Oh well, what's done is done. I will just need to be more careful. I wasn't going to stay here much longer anyway. My twelve week commitment was drawing to a close, and following Labor Day, park visitors would rapidly decrease. Normally, I headed to my home in McMinnville during this hiatus. I would have headed home earlier but didn't want to draw attention to myself by doing that, so I simply changed my commitment for a change of scene, which volunteers often did. That all sounded like a good plan, so I finished my ice water, got up, put on a coat and went for a walk on the beach, during which I decided to keep things suburban for now. Dealing with the cameras and the big city was something I didn't want to tackle just yet.

Chapter 38

The police found Jenny Carter's body two days later. She had been assaulted, then strangled. They found her pathetic little body off the side of the road by a search party two miles from her home. The Police Chief fought back tears as he gave this news to Jenny's parents, and then to the public.

Chapter 39

Data from the children's bodies, clothing and accessories made quite a pile. The cause of death for most of Johnny Fields' victims was pretty consistent. Rape and torture on the mattress in the basement, all of which were fully documented for future viewing. During the morning briefing with the task force, it was suggested the videos were made to sell online to a further selection of perverts. The task force leader assigned researching that angle to the detective who suggested it. Perhaps it would lead to an audience of snuff films, although that wasn't heard about a lot these days. Still, it required looking into.

Otherwise, finding the parents or guardians of these children was taking form. The police had already found one couple, and they established a hotline for parents seeking their missing children. In addition, a couple officers diligently worked to match missing children with the evidence found at the scene.

The forensics department still worked on site at the Fields crime scene. Each room in the house, and the property itself, had its own story to tell about what happened here. The actual story behind the property looked pretty straightforward. Fields had an aunt and uncle, who were very fond of the boy. When they died, they left him the house and everything in it. Very simple. During his child molestation trials, Johnny's ownership of the house was not taken into account.

The title transfer may have occurred after Johnny's conviction. Something else to be researched. Anderson was grateful that closure was coming to the families of these children, but he was sad that so many children suffered at the hands of Johnny Fields. What were these young kids thinking as Johnny abused them? Where's my mom? I want to go home? Stop, you're hurting me. It was just too much to dwell on, too painful.

Johnny's part in this scenario had ended. Anderson was glad about that. But he couldn't stop thinking about the caller who notified them of this travesty. Who was he? What was his game? Was he the guy who called earlier those other times? Anderson wished he knew the answer. It was unfortunate that he had to bring this guy in. He could understand the man's rage at what he uncovered. But what was he doing there in the first place? Who was he? So many questions with no answers. His phone chirped loudly, jolting Anderson out of his reveille. He picked up the phone.

"Anderson here," he said.

"Hello, Lieutenant. It's Sheryl. We're almost done here. Probably finish tomorrow. We've had pretty decent luck finding the families of these kids. There's only a couple we're still working on."

"OK, Sheryl. Thanks for letting me know." He hung up the phone. By now he was totally burned out and just wanted to go home and relax with a beer. He logged out of his computer, grabbed his jacket, and headed home.

CHAPTER 40

I was on the road again, using the addresses given me by the sex offender database I used for my list. I approached the home of Oscar Milton. Oscar was an odd duck. He looked the typical nerd stereotype. Dressed in tweeds, wore a bow tie. Glasses. That was all a disguise, meant to lure younger children into a false sense of friendship. His antics mimicked in some ways a popular kiddy show host, which was intentional. Children liked him. Parents liked him. He was very charming. But, if you checked some data bases back east, it would show Oscar had a penchant for little blond girls. He liked to watch them. He liked to touch them.

He would inure himself with the children and their guardians, so much so they often dropped their guard and allowed him access to their children. Then he would offer to babysit, or tutor children or some such other activity. After a while, the child might say something or complain about something to the mother or the father. When what he did to these children behind closed doors came to light, Oscar would disappear before they could apprehend him, starting anew in another location. The police arrested him several times. The courts convicted him once. Oscar was supposed to register as a sex offender but rarely did when bouncing around the States. Consequently, background checks revealed little of Oscar's sordid past and he just kept on torturing and abusing children. Until one day...

I tripped over Oscar's name while searching the sex offender database. The file contained little information, but its contents appeared peculiar, prompting me to access the record. "Guilty of misdemeanor something or other, blah, blah, blah. Hmm, he's near here. I think I'll check him out."

I jotted down his address as one to visit. Oscar's address and a couple of others fit into my plan to check them all out. I stood up from the dinette table with my laptop, stretched, and got a drink of water. Grabbing a banana from the kitchen counter, I headed out to the truck.

Now I was a block from Oscar's house. And it didn't appear that Oscar was home. Good break for me. Oscar's absence during the early afternoon hinted at his work schedule. I hadn't bothered to find out. He lived pretty close to the park where I was working, so I just drove by the area. As I drove down the street, I noticed that there were hardly any people around. Most people also probably still at work. Excellent. I pulled over and parked the truck down the street from his house. Because I couldn't tell if anyone on the street was home or not, I grabbed a clipboard with some nondescript papers on it I had placed in the truck, intending to act like a utility worker if approached. Of course, all the papers were bogus, but as long as someone didn't look too close, I should be able to pass muster. Walking up to the front door, I knocked. There didn't appear to be any cameras around or a one of those fancy ring camera doorbells. When no one answered the front door, I went around to where all the utility hookups were and acted like I was reading the meter. Surreptitiously, I looked around and could see no one. With that, I stood and moved to the back of the house. In the back and along the sides of the house was a long row of arborvitae, acting as a visual barrier. Once back there, I became completely invisible from the rest of the neighborhood. Back here was a patio door and a couple windows, plus a back door to the garage. But everything was locked tight, which frustrated me. Then I saw a rock lying in a garden that had an odd color. I picked it up and discovered it was a cheap attempt at one of those rocks with a key inside. I opened it and Voila! A key was present. It was quick work to remove the key, insert it into the garage door, and the door opened inward.

I crept in, waiting to hear an alarm, or maybe a dog, but nothing assailed me. Moving past the door, I closed it behind me. Next, I reached the door from the garage into the house and stepped inside. The door opened into the kitchen, which, although neat and tidy, was pretty small. I didn't expect to find anything in the kitchen, so I moved into the rest of the house, taking care to stay away from the windows.

After the kitchen was a small dining room, more of a breakfast nook. Beige carpet covered the living room and presumably the rest of the house except for the bathrooms, while the kitchen and dining room had tiles. Oscar's solitary lifestyle was evident from his living room, which was comprised of a single overstuffed chair positioned in front of the television. It was an off brand sixty five inch flat screen sitting on a TV display stand. Underneath on the stand were a DVD player and the setup for a home theater system. All of it looked mediocre quality. Oscar was obviously a cheap bastard, even on himself. Oh well, not my problem. A small table stood at the back of the room with pictures and things on it. There appeared to be a drawer under the table, so I opened it and carefully went through the items there, trying my best not to disturb anything and put it back the way I found it.

The desk drawer yielded nothing, so I proceeded down a hallway that led to the bedrooms. The first room was pretty small and used as an office. Before I examined the computer there, I went to the other room and checked it out. It boasted a queen-sized bed, a chest of drawers, a nightstand, and an overstuffed chair that matched the one in the living room. A floor lamp stood just behind the chair to illuminate over the shoulder. The nightstand held some suggestive magazines, but nothing overly incriminating. The last item I noticed was a small bedside lamp. I went back to the office and sat at the desk before the computer.

Here, no expense was spared. The computer was a high end gaming computer and looked very robust. His monitor screen was a forty inch Samsung 4D curved unit, maybe even larger. I cautiously turned the computer on. It booted up quickly, not even password protected. Then again, my computer in the trailer wasn't protected either. *Maybe I should change that*, I thought.

Oscar was a narcissistic fool. In plain sight, right on the desktop, he had an icon marked Special. I tapped it and a host of photographs and videos burst to the surface. Awful pictures of children doing horrible things. I saw Oscar frolicking naked with one, sometimes two, children. Some photos had them outside somewhere, dancing in a meadow surrounded by trees. It turned my stomach. Oscar didn't seem to be a killer, for which

I was grateful. Despite that, he had to be taken care of. But how to make it look like an accident? I could do the gas thing again, but that seemed prone to discovery. Slip in the shower, maybe? Overcome by fumes in the garage? Maybe an accidental overdose of some pills? I kind of liked that one, but I did not know if he took anything possibly dangerous. I got up to check the medicine chest in the bathroom. The medicine chest hung on the wall over the sink. I opened the medicine chest door but didn't find anything I could use. How was I going to do this?

The idea slowly came to me about a burglary gone bad. That seemed to be the easiest solution with the circumstances at hand. I could easily dodge Oscar to avoid leaving any proof behind and make it look like a break in. I had my gun so I could shoot Oscar, take some money or something, maybe his computer, and then leave. This was if I wanted to do the job myself and I was already here. It seemed like the only option at this point.

I wasn't too fond of this idea because it meant I had to wait until Oscar came back home. But there didn't seem to be any other choice. I wanted this taken care of. Tonight. I sat down to wait.

Oscar never came home. On the way to a meeting at a bar to discuss gaming with his friends, an SUV ran a stoplight and t-boned his car. Oscar was life flighted to the nearest hospital where he died of his injuries. I waited a couple of hours before I gave up and decided to go home and try again later. It was on the news that night that Oscar was in an accident and later died. It was hard for me to feel sad, except for maybe the other driver. I was going to kill Oscar myself and this saved me the trouble, plus it helped to muddy up the waters and obscure my activities from the police. I ate my dinner watching television, content with the news.

Chapter 41

Lieutenant Anderson sat at his desk, mulling over the report on Johnny Fields. The case was moving along, except for any evidence leading to the vigilante killer. They found shoe prints outside the kitchen window, but they were very faint and found in the grass. Unlikely they would be of any use. Best they could do were snapshots. A cast of the shoe print wasn't possible. That was all they had. No fingerprints, no hair, no shell casings, nothing on anything. It was clear there was a struggle, and Johnny lost. The killer must have wiped everything down before he left.

Nothing leading up to the house either. Several officers combed the woods, hoping to find any trace of the killer, but they could find nothing definitive.

Their only clue, and a thin one at that, was the series of phone calls Anderson received. The calls informed him of a child predator working at a grade school, and then a reaming out by the same guy when Jordan Knightly went missing. Could they possibly be the same person as the one who called about Johnny? He reached for the intercom.

"Jack, you there?" A moment's silence, then an electronic click. "Yes, sir?"

"Come in here a minute, please."

"Be right there," said Jack. A moment later, Jack arrived carrying two cups of coffee. As he handed one to Anderson, Anderson acknowledged his thanks and motioned for Jack to sit. Jack dropped into the chair in front of Lieutenant Anderson's desk, placing his coffee at the edge of the desk within easy reach. "What's up?" he asked. Anderson frowned at him, using slang. Jack grinned sheepishly. "Sorry, sir. Kids at home are corrupting me."

Anderson chuckled. "I know what you mean. Anyway, I want to talk some more about this Johnny Fields case." Jack took a sip of his coffee.

"Okay, what were you thinking?" Jack asked.

"I'm building a hunch. Let me bounce this off you. We get a call from a concerned citizen that a convicted child molester is working at an elementary school in violation of his parole. How did this citizen know that? Second, he makes another call after Jordan Knightly's murder, and it turns out that Bateman, whom this person had warned us about, is the killer. Now, we get a third call, out of the blue, that a child predator has been murdered by the person on the phone. Further, this caller tells us there are dead kids buried in the backyard of this person he has just killed. Is it the same person on all three calls? We don't have any tapes for any voice comparison, do we?"

Jack shifted in his seat. "No sir, I don't believe we do. He never stays on the phone long enough to get a sample." Anderson leaned back in his creaking office chair, staring at the ceiling for a moment. Jack waited patiently, sipping his coffee. He knew this was how his boss worked. Finally, Anderson leaned forward, his chair protesting the movement.

"Let's pull a list of all deceased child predators in Oregon, Washington, California, and Idaho. Maybe we are in unfamiliar territory, or maybe our boy has been working here for a while and we didn't notice. Can do?"

"Sure, Lieutenant, I can do that. Might be an extensive list, though."

"No problem. Grab one of the interns to help you. Maybe one of them that helped plug all that data into VICAP. Can you get it to me tomorrow morning before the briefing?"

"Shouldn't be any problem, sir. Especially with some help. I'll get right on it." Jack gulped the rest of his coffee down, then stood up, making for the office door.

"Great," said Anderson. "Any questions come see me or call me."

"Will do."

Chapter 42

I was overjoyed to know Oscar had gone to meet his maker. Good riddance. One less creep for me to worry about.

A few campers were checking out today, so I wouldn't be able to get to the other predators on my list until later. While making my breakfast, I listened to the news, which again briefly covered Oscar's demise, then moved on to other stories, both local and national.

After I finished my coffee, I sauntered over to the rangers' office to pick up my golf cart and supplies. After that, and chatting with other camp volunteers over another cup of coffee, it was time to patrol the sites, looking to restore the campsites to their original pristine status. One of my assignments had already checked out, so I headed that direction and was soon picking up bits of trash, gathering leftover firewood, maybe moving the picnic table back to its original position. Sometimes the fire ring needed ashes removed. It was all pretty lightweight stuff, and it relaxed me. The next site after that was a yurt. These units are pretty cool. The walls and ceiling are a canvas wrap over a wooden lattice affair, set on a raised dais. The corkscrew mechanism on the ceiling allows you to open or shut a plastic bubble overhead, An enclosed metal key with a large hole in it would accept a hooked pole device operated by the yurt tenant. By operating the pole clockwise or counterclockwise, the bubble would raise up or down, helping to control air flow.

A wooden door with a deadbolt and plastic screened windows were part of the yurt's features. The plastic coverings over the windows could be fastened back to allow air to flow at ground level as well. The floor of these units was typically tiled over a subfloor suspended a foot or so off the ground to prevent rot and bugs. One thing these units didn't come with was air conditioning, so if exposed to the sun, they could get hot. They came with a heater though, so you wouldn't freeze during the winter months. Each unit came furnished with a bunkbed arrangement, a fold down futon, a small table, a lamp, and two chairs. They were pretty self-sufficient. The unit provided one or two electrical outlets for personal use, such as charging electronics or using a radio. Outside was a porch with a gabled roof overhead to protect you from the rain. A hardwood bench was part of the porch as well. Out in the campsite were a picnic bench and a fire ring. Between the next site was a single water spigot. All in all, a neat setup.

Unit A was ahead of me. I unlocked the door and stepped inside. The occupants, now gone, were responsible campers. A fresh plastic bag was lining the trash can. The place looked ready to go after I swept the floor. Still, park protocol insisted I wipe everything down and sweep yet again. It was a simple procedure and only took a few minutes. I could see advantages to the procedure. Wiping down and sweeping as a matter of course eliminated any concern of uncleanliness coming from the next users of the yurt. No guesswork was involved. We appreciate the fact users emptied the garbage and swept the floor, but we still need to wipe everything down anyway, so why not sweep as well, just to be sure?

Once finished with the yurt, I packed things up and made a sweep by my other sites, but they were still occupied. Checkout time was one pm, and it was early yet. The management didn't strictly enforce the checkout time. A very relaxed way of operating. Since I had time on my hands, I drove around the sites, stopping occasionally to answer questions from campers, pickup any loose litter, making myself useful.

Finally, about midafternoon, all my units were cleaned and ready to receive new campers. I checked in with the office for any last assignments, then made my way to the trailer to relax. I had work to do that night, and I wanted to be ready.

Chapter 43

Molly's abductor had come and gone several times now. At first he was somewhat gentle, relatively speaking, and he only hurt her a little. He never said much, but she gathered she was some sort of surrogate replacement for his sister, who had died. The story went he felt unnaturally attracted to her apparently, and one night he could no longer stand it, and he came to her room. She resisted his advances. In a blind rage he slapped her, hard.

He was a big man, and she was petite. The force of the blow whipped her around and she fell off the bed, striking her head on the chest of drawers and died. He opened up to Molly one time early in the repeated rapes, expressing his incestuous love for his sister and her subsequent rejection of him, setting up a dangerous psychotic paradox within his psyche. Molly gleaned all this from what little he said during his visits. He never mentioned his parents, and Molly was afraid to ask about them.

He clearly meant for her to keep herself clean. Taking her to the bathroom when she asked, kept her fed, although the food was mediocre and typically takeout. He brought her clothes Molly suspected were his sisters, because of the style. But they were fresh and clean, which Molly was grateful for.

During his last visit, things seemed to change. He seemed distracted and had trouble satisfying himself. When he finished, he immediately rolled off her and stood over her like the first time. And again, like the first time, he slugged her hard, this time in the stomach. She lay there gasping with pain, struggling to catch her breath as he leaned over her.

"You did that on purpose. You're trying to keep me from being happy!" he said. He slapped her then. "Stop it!" he screamed. Then he marched out, slamming the door behind him. Molly couldn't figure out what she had done. She desperately wanted to keep him happy. She didn't know what he would do if he became really angry.

CHAPTER 44

I sat in a shopping mall parking lot, going over my list and plugging the addresses into the GPS system I used for the truck. It wasn't built into the entertainment electronics for the truck like OnStar, but was a separate device I purchased years ago when Grace and I first started traveling. I kept the maps up to date and used it to find my way across the United States. The item could be destroyed if the authorities caught up to me before I finished, since I did not link it to the truck's electronics.

I went to plug in an address when a dull, familiar pain burned in my gut, and I had an awful feeling that my old nemesis was back. Well, it would have to wait because I had business to attend to. Thomas Carlyle was my next target. I put the truck in gear and headed for his house. Tonight was just a stake out night, if I could manage it. I wasn't one to jump in to something without a plan, usually. Johnny was the only one so far where I killed him off the cuff, so to speak. Life had intervened and Johnny was dead. For which I was glad. I reached Carlyle's home. The place was spacious. Two stories, a circular driveway, many windows. Lots of yard. It was almost a compound, which would mean cameras. Maybe lots of cameras.

But as I turned down his street, I saw lots of cars parked everywhere. I neared the house and could hear loud music carry across the lawn. A party was evidently underway. It intrigued me. The party posed a problem, but possibly an opportunity. Thomas was one of those bastards that floated through the system, sliding by on technicalities. He was rich; he had competent lawyers, and he was connected. Nothing seemed to stick to him. But I had discovered enough on him to be sure he was an active predator, abusing underage girls in the dark behind closed doors, possibly during parties, just like this one. But maybe, just maybe, tonight his luck would change.

People were still arriving, it being early evening. Many people were walking toward the house. Some dressed up, but enough dressed casually that my attire wouldn't attract too much attention. I decided to go in to check things out. If I found a sport jacket or a sweater I could grab, even better. Man, I was turning into a real James Bond!

I parked out in the street and made my way toward the house. Nearing the house, I checked for cameras. A few existed, but were poorly placed. I'd watched enough movies and TV dramas to know more than these guys how to place cameras to eliminate dead spots. If Carlyle had a security team, they were doing a piss-poor job of protecting him.

I moved further into the house to find people everywhere. Buffet tables stood along one wall and incredibly delightful smells of steak, crab, and lobster on the barbecue made my mouth water and reminded me it had been hours since I ate. This realization led me to head for the food and drink.

As I piled my plate with food, I used the moment to check out the people, hoping to find Thomas. His picture was on the predator database, so I knew what he looked like. I spotted him off to one side, but I didn't like what I saw. A tall, thin sort of guy, with curly hair and a quick smile. Arrogant. Confident. He laughed a lot. He was talking to a group of middle-aged men. What seemed odd was the young girl standing by his side. She looked nervous, a little scared, yet eager to be in a room full of sophisticated people. She couldn't be over sixteen. I looked at this group and images of child trafficking came to mind. I couldn't believe it. *Damn it, no! Were all these people predators? Or just innocent bystanders? How would you know?* The thought of what might happen tonight involving that girl made me sick to my stomach. My intention was to prevent it from happening, but I wasn't going to act carelessly like with Johnny. I intended to stick around, avoid the cameras and the people if I could, and punch Tommy's ticket if I got the chance. I absolutely wasn't going to let him put his hands on that young girl.

I settled in a chair placed in one corner and devoured the meats, fruits and breads I placed on the plate. But the food had lost its flavor, and I ate now to replenish my energy level. Even with the nap I took earlier, I still felt tired. Now I knew why. My cancer had returned. After finishing my food, I kept my eating utensils in my pocket in case anyone checked for fingerprints. Then I moved out to the deck in the backyard. Set up in the backyard was a small band. They may have been small, but the volume of their music was impressive. They weren't too bad. The backyard was huge, with lots of flower gatherings and trees. I couldn't help but wonder what might lie below the trees near the back of the yard.

The party began winding up as more arrived. Earlier, I snagged a coat from the back of one chair and now looked indistinguishable from the other guests. I even danced a few times with pretty ladies to fit in. All the while, I kept watch on Thomas and his escort, if you will. After a few dances, I moved off and, under the disguise of needing a bathroom, used the excuse to move about the house, ostensibly with the excuse that most of the bathrooms were in use.

Climbing the stairs to the upper floor, I discovered the master bedroom. My instincts told me this would be where Thomas brought her. It lay at the end of a hallway, away from the guests. Making sure no one was watching, I slipped into the room, softly closing the bedroom door behind me. It looked very opulent, with fine drapes framing the patio door. Expensive paintings adorned all four walls. At least they looked expensive, I wouldn't know. An oversized bed occupied one wall, a couple of overstuffed chairs were scattered around a coffee table, and a chest of drawers with a mirror on top of it furnished the room tastefully. Against one wall, a small table filled with alcohol bottles. I could see the bathroom door in a small alcove. A large screen TV dominated the wall at the foot of the bed, arranged so you could watch it while reclined. And the usual high end home theater system rested within an audio cabinet below the TV. That struck me as odd, because another cabinet stood like a protective soldier next to the entrance of the walk-in closet. Now what was that cabinet for? I had a sneaky, nasty thought, and I looked to open the door to the cabinet, but found it locked.

That raised my hackles even more, so I looked around for a key, and found it in a small ornamental box resting on the nightstand next to the bed. My suspicions were justified when I opened the door and found the prerequisite recording equipment, along with recording media of DVD's and flash drives. This Thomas character must have quite a collection of private home porn. What was even worse was I found tablets and vials of several opioids, some heroin, even a little pot to round out the selection. God, was this guy going to drug the girl and then rape her? It appeared likely. From what I saw downstairs, the girl was pretty scared, which led me to believe that possibly this may not be voluntary.

Just as I discovered this treasure trove of perverted happiness, I heard noises in the hall. I shut off the light and dove into the walk-in closet, secreting myself back behind the clothes and praying not to be discovered. Lights came on in the room, and I could hear Thomas ushering in his fun for the night with an arm around her waist. I decided right then and there that was not going to happen, even if I had to expose myself and have my mission come to an abrupt end. Who did these rich people think they were, using young girls as their play toys? I almost marched out right then, but decided to wait and see if a better chance presented itself.

"Make yourself comfortable, my dear," said the slimy bastard, who would soon be dead.

"Let me fix you something to drink."

The young girl stepped into the room, looking around at all the fine things scattered in the room, then sat down on the couch. She wore a pretty blue short-sleeved frock with black heels. "Wow," she said. "This is so awesome." She looked dazed, a nervous look on her face. "Thank you, sir," she said. "But I am underage," she admitted. Thomas was at the bar, fixing the drink. I kept my eye on him and sure enough, he palmed a small tablet into the glass, then filled the glass with a mix of rum and soda. Done with that, he picked up the glass and moved to her, handing her the drink.

"I won't say anything if you won't," he said with a greasy smile. "Let's just relax and enjoy ourselves." He took a sip of his drink, then motioned to her to do the same with hers. She looked at the drink in her lap, then raised the glass and took a small sip. She promptly made a face.

"Ugh!" she said. "That tastes awful!" Thomas gave a short laugh.

"Ha! Dear. Take a few more sips and you'll see it tastes better and better with each sip. Go on, try another." She took another sip, and then whatever he had slipped into her drink began to take effect.

"Mmm, I see what you mean. This tastes nice." She took another sip, a bigger one this time. "I like it," she murmured.

About this time, I could see that Thomas was about to make his move. He already had a few in his system and he was eager to party. He was now sitting on the couch next to this girl and pressed into her forcefully, covering her lips with his own. The girl, caught off guard, spilled a portion of her drink onto the carpet.

"Wait a minute, I'm not ready for this. I just wanted to have a drink," she said. She pushed away from him and tried to stand up, but he grabbed her and pulled her roughly to the couch.

"Who do you think you are, you little bitch?! Did you really think all we came in here to do was drink and watch TV? Maybe have some popcorn and watch cartoons? I don't think so! Come here!"

She squirmed and tried to get out from underneath him, but he wrapped one leg over her and held her hands above her head with one hand, while the other explored her chest and then moved down under her skirt.

"Stop! Let me go! Stop, you're hurting me!" she cried, struggling against him.

"Oh, you're going to be great. I just know it. This is going to be epic!" cried Thomas.

About then I reached Thomas. The couch was facing away from me, so I came up behind him and coldcocked him with a decanter of scotch taken from the table. Miraculously, it didn't break, and he slumped forward, rolling off her and onto the floor, laying on his back. The young girl lay there and burst into tears. That was okay with me. With her eyes closed and her face turned away, I gambled she wouldn't get a visual of me. Now I had to figure out what to do with Thomas, and how to get the girl out of here.

I already decided how I was going to kill Thomas. In a ridiculously easy way. He had a supply of fentanyl pills in his cache in the cabinet. I mixed several of these with water and gave him a massive dose through injection. I fully expected him to stop breathing in a few minutes and go into hypoxia. This could easily lead to a coma, or, I hoped, death. With this done, I now turned to the girl.

She hadn't swallowed too much of what Thomas spiked her drink with, which was good, as I wanted her to get out of here under her own power. I left her laying on the couch as I set the room up to expose Thomas and his friends. Whatever was going on here stank, and I was going to shut it down.

Once that was done, I moved to the girl on the couch. She didn't look asleep, just drowsy and coasting on the drugs. I sat on the couch next to her and gently shook her. "Hey, wake up. It's time to go," I said to her. "We've got to get out of here." She slowly came to, a bewildered look on her face.

"Where am I? Wait! Someone was trying to rape me!" Her eyes got wide, and she started moving away from me. I held up a hand.

"Not me," I said, pointing to Thomas on the ground. "Him." She looked down at Thomas on the floor, her mind processing the last few moments of consciousness. I didn't want her to get too awake. "Come on, someone is going to check on what's going on in here and we need to be gone."

I stood up and moved to the back wall of the bedroom, which had drapes drawn across it. Sweeping them back, I saw a patio door that led to a balcony. I stepped out and looked around outside. The main party was at the other end of the house, so this area was private, discreet, with no observers. I noticed a flight of stairs leading from the balcony to the ground below. Large arborvitae marked the border of the backyard, but a small gate stood near the bottom of the stairs. "Well, that is certainly convenient." I said to myself. "Perfect."

I returned to the room and found the girl sitting up, but still droopy, her eyes half closed. I helped her up to a standing position. She wobbled a bit, then caught her balance.

"I'm ok," she said. Her eyes were downcast as she stared at the carpet. "Thanks for saving me." I put an arm around her.

"He put something in your drink. I saw him do it. Who knows what he was planning to do to you? Listen, we need to get out of here, and I need a favor from you." She looked up at him.

"What favor is that?" she questioned. I started pulling her toward the balcony door.

"Let's get downstairs first." She moved with me and we moved out to the balcony and then down the steps. I quickly had us get to the gate and then we were out and both safe. I turned to her. "Here's what I want. Do you have a cell phone? Of course you do. What teenage girl doesn't? I want you to wait for about ten minutes and then call the police. Tell them what's going on here, and that Thomas tried to rape you. You escaped and called them.

I was never here, okay? They can't know I was involved. Can you do that for me?" She nodded, then turned to go.

"Thanks, mister, whoever you are."

I watched her move down the street and then made my way back around to the front of the house to where the cars were parked. I found my truck and started her up, pulling quietly out and moving down the street.

That evening, the local evening news broke the story of a party gone bad where several prominent people were arrested. The morning news reported the death by overdose of Thomas Carlyle, a local bigwig in the community. The news anchors talked of a possible investigation into illicit drugs and other things, but the story was too new to have a lot of detail.

CHAPTER 45

It thrilled me that my escapade had a happy conclusion, at least for me. I never learned the girl's name, but I wished her the best and sincerely hoped she learned a lesson from her near rape experience.

It was after I got to the trailer that the burn from my cancer began again, seeping into my organs. The excitement of the evening made the pain more intense, agonizing even, to the point I took one of Doc's pain pills and sat in my chair, waiting for the pain to pass. It eventually did, but by then I was a weak kitten and crawled to my bed and crashed, not even bothering to undress.

The next day, I felt drained and decided to back my schedule off a little and rest. No sites were scheduled to be cleaned today, so I sat outside my trailer, basking in the sun, just enjoying life. How much longer I could keep this up, I didn't know. Frankly, I was surprised my mission was lasting as long as it had. I must be doing a pretty good job of covering up my tracks. Anyway, I dozed in the sun for a few hours, protected from the direct rays by the awning stretched out over me. It was a nice day.

CHAPTER 46

He was coming again, soon. Molly could feel it. She was getting worried. Three times now he had labored to complete his rape. Each episode was more extreme than the last. He blamed her for his struggles, and she was sure that unless something changed, he would soon kill her. As it sat, she now sported a black eye, a split lip and sore ribs. He kicked her once and a large bruise formed on her thigh.

The handcuffs chaffed her wrists and ankles when she struggled, and now abrasions and bleeding could be added to her condition. She was getting weaker as well. He wanted her to be like his first time. Energetic, feisty, screaming, but she just didn't have the strength anymore. She knew she wouldn't last much longer. Something had to change.

Chapter 47

It came to pass that my cancer symptoms overrode my desire to terminate the monsters that crossed my path. From the pain itself to the side effects of my pain pills, it was clear I was in no shape to continue for now. The year was getting on and it was time for me to return to McMinnville, Oregon, where I lived off season. It was my cue to depart from the park, so everything fell into place.

I said my goodbyes to the rangers and park hosts, promised to see them next year, which wasn't likely, and headed west towards the coast. I had half a mind to visit my son in Redding, California, so that's how I planned my trip. It was kind of a long way around, but after Redding I could take highway 299 and visit some national and state parks, like Redwood National and Prairie Creek forests. These were favorite spots Grace and I enjoyed. And, since I resolutely believed my time was short, I wanted to see them one last time.

I called my son's cell phone intending to announce my coming, but he told me they were in Italy for a combination business trip slash vacation and wouldn't be home when I would pass through. He asked me if anything was wrong, but I assured him everything was fine. I just wanted to visit. I didn't want to spoil his trip, as it was obvious from background noise that Rebecca, his wife, and the two boys, Logan and Lucas, were having a great time in the hotel pool. Everybody chatted with me over the phone, then I wished them well and hung up. I didn't know if there would be another opportunity for us to get together. That was too bad.

I stopped at his house in Redding just to have a memory and then headed out of Redding on Highway 299. Towards Whiskeytown National Recreation Area. Once there, I pulled in, paid my fee and set up camp in the late afternoon. Since I was only spending the one night again, it wasn't worth it to pay for a full hookup. Leaving the truck hitched to the trailer, I went inside. I was in a foul mood for some reason. Maybe because I wouldn't be able to see the boys or my son. It had been too long. Also, the pain was creeping in again. I didn't wait so long this time and took my pain pill right away, which helped quite a bit. The pill had a drowsy side effect, and it wasn't long before I fell asleep watching a movie on TV.

Chapter 48

I woke up the next morning feeling better, but weak. For a change of pace, I ate oatmeal with some fruit and toast, as well as my standard coffee. The drain on my body from the pain pills was much like my diabetic lows. Everything was in a fog and I couldn't think. I've had lows so bad I couldn't figure out the remote for my TV. Now that's bad; a few steps from a diabetic coma. But here I was today, still functioning.

Because of my attack last night, I took my time getting ready and pulled out from the park right at checkout time again headed down Highway 299, known as Eureka Way, for home via the coast highway system. As the day wore on, I felt much better and began to enjoy the ride home. After learning I wouldn't meet up with Robert and his family, my enthusiasm faded for a visit to the forests, but I continued because I knew I would enjoy the drive up the coast.

It was an inspiring drive, winding through the hills, passing through small towns, one after the other, some old and run down, others providing needed services in strategic places. I even ate a late lunch at a small restaurant in one of these towns, and they impressed me with the quality of the food. How did they do that way out here?

Although I was determined to reach the coast before I stopped for the night, it got to be so late I finally pulled off the side of the road and called it done. I was a little nervous about this, being out in the sticks, but I had done this many times and had protection with me, along with the proper licenses and permits to carry it, so I wasn't too worried. That was good, because where I stopped the cell service was zilch. I would have taken my dinner outside, but the wind picked up and the temperature dropped rather quickly and the night turned chilly. I opened the windows a bit to refresh the inside air of the trailer. Placing my dinner plate in front of me, I sat down at the computer to see what my connection speed might be. The satellite signal was strong and good enough for me to log on, though not great. I logged on and pulled up MSN, catching up with the news. Still the same old shit, different day. After a while, I tired of this and settled down with my book. In about a half an hour, my lids were heavy, and I got up and went to the bathroom. After putting on my pajamas, I splashed water on my face, brushed my teeth, and crawled into bed.

After breakfast the next morning I took my coffee outside to take in the sights, which admittedly were less than stellar. Some dry grass, trees, and an occasional squirrel. A hawk soared overhead, looking for a meal. A few cars and recreational vehicles drove by as well. That was about it. I finished my coffee and went back inside the trailer, washed the breakfast dishes, and made sure everything was secure inside the trailer. I stepped out, locked the trailer, and climbed into the truck cab. The truck started easily and I eased out onto the highway, continuing my quest to get to the coast.

The drive was much the same as yesterday, curving through the mountains and driving through small towns slowly dying. Only a few hours remained before I reached Highway 101 and my turnoff for McMinnville. Since it was still early, I continued up Highway 101, enjoying the view of the Pacific Ocean. Upon reaching the Redwood parks, I drove through the magnificent trees towering in to the sky. The experience was totally glorious.

Once I reached Crescent City, I pulled into the Ramblin Redwoods Campground. Again, I only intended to stay the one night, so I paid for a non-hook up site, pulled into my assigned space and unhooked the trailer from the truck. On my way in, I noticed a big box chain store and thought I could stock up on some things for the trailer and a few things I would need immediately once I got to my house. The time was late evening, and the hint of some dark clouds promising rain lay above the horizon, heading slowly towards me. I estimated it would rain in a couple of hours. I pulled into the store's parking lot. Once inside the store I grabbed a shopping cart, wiped it down with some disinfectant, a habit Grace instilled in me years back, and made my way into the store. It would be late afternoon by the time I reached my house tomorrow, and I preferred not to cook the following morning once I was home. I intended to crash and relax for a day before resuming the life of a homeowner. Browsing through the store, I picked up milk, breakfast food, coffee, bread, some vegetables, water, diet soda, and the essential ice cream.

I was in the checkout lane, unloading my shopping cart and placing the items on the conveyor belt, when I felt an icy presence unexpectedly touch me. As though a freezing cold cloud moved down my spine. I stopped unloading my goods onto the conveyor belt and looked around. In the next lane over, I saw him.

I am not an overly religious man, but I believe in evil. It walks among us in several forms and disguises, often fooling people with a cloak of confusion. Many people can and are deceived by it. I was not one of them. Perhaps my dealings with the lowest scum of the earth from living with a social worker and looking death right in the face sensitized me to these demons, so I was not taken in. The cold flush embraced me again after I looked at this man. I could hardly move.

I surveyed his face, partially turned from me as he unloaded his choices onto the belt. He was tall, taller than me by a couple inches, with dark hair. His face, from the side anyway, looked neither exceptionally handsome nor ugly. A non-descript face, void of emotion. He smiled at the clerk, but the smile didn't exist past his lips. The eyes seemed dead, as if no soul inhabited his body. The body hidden under his clothes appeared soft, weak, and he fumbled while moving, unsure of his place among us humans. He was true evil personified.

"Sir, that's forty-two dollars and seventy four cents? Sir?"

The clerk for my lane startled me, speaking to me. It brought me to my senses, and I paid the young man with bills from my pocket. Once the transaction was complete, I moved out of the way for the next customer, moving up to a wall by the customer service desk, pretending to check my receipt. I watched this demon from hell finish his business with the clerk and move his cart out, heading for the exit.

For whatever reason I followed him, carefully observing his every move. He sauntered slowly out into the parking lot toward an old Dodge Neon sedan. My truck was just an aisle over and down a couple, so I hurried to my truck, unlocked the door and climbed in, still watching him. I placed my groceries on the front passenger seat next to me and waited for the demon to finish depositing his load in the Neon. He climbed into the driver's seat, started the car, and backed out. I backed out too, making sure to act like I just happened to be going his way. He exited from the parking lot, turning right and driving down the street, out of town. I followed in my truck, keeping a couple car lengths between us. But I was getting concerned. The fading light and overcast sky made it difficult to spot his car. I finally turned my lights on as others were doing as well. At last, his taillights lit up and I caught a break; one tail light was out. It became much easier to keep track of him after that.

He was a few miles out of town when he turned onto a side street that led down a suburban road of track homes that had no outlet. He kept going until he reached the end, where a large home stood in what appeared to be a multi-acre lot. It looked to be a Cape Cod style, painted white, with dormers on the second floor straddling the front door on the first. I held back as he pulled into the driveway, the garage door opening as he came to a stop. He climbed out of the car and opened up the back door of the sedan to grab his groceries. He pressed a button on the garage wall and the door began descending. I saw him move inside the house, and that's when I got out of my truck and walked toward the home. There was something wrong about all this, but I couldn't place it. I had a feeling in my stomach that something was off. Keeping to the grass, I edged up to the house, trying to catch a sound of where he was. There was something eerie about the house.

The windows looked funny, not quite right. Some kids were playing in the cul-de-sac in front of the house and the echoes bouncing off the siding sounded flat, as though the house was super dense, absorbing noises, not reflecting them back. I pulled out my favorite weapon, a forty-five caliber Bersa semi-automatic concealed in a conceal carry waist holster, and chambered a round. I was determined to find out what was going on here. Things could escalate pretty fast, so I needed to be ready. Wait, what was that? I cocked my head to one side, straining to catch a faint sound…

CHAPTER 49

Weak from exhaustion and the beatings her abductor gave her, Molly heard the turn of the key in the lock and knew the monster had returned. She felt him enter the house, then place groceries she imagined on the kitchen table she saw when moving toward the bathroom. The bedroom door swung inward, and in he came with the usual toiletries and change of clothes. Tonight, he was brusque, short with her. He stood over her and unlocked her chains. Molly stood up from the bed, knowing that before he assaulted her, he allowed her to go to the bathroom and get herself somewhat presentable. Molly was so tired; she didn't know why she bothered; it didn't matter. He would still have his way with her. When finished, he would rest a second, then get up and start beating her. It was too much. She couldn't take any more. What was she going to do?

"Come on," he said, gesturing with the pile in his hand. "Get on in there. I haven't got all night, bitch." She moved from the bed out into the hall, heading down towards the bathroom. She entered the bathroom and used the toilet, but she was doing it less frequently because of dehydration. After starting the shower, she removed the few pieces of clothing he allowed her to keep. As she stepped into the shower, the doorbell rang, and she froze. Oh my God, she thought. Someone's here. Someone's here. SOMEONES'S HERE!!!! She opened her mouth and began screaming.

Chapter 50

I often heard a good defense was a strong offense. I pressed the doorbell firmly, trying to form my thoughts into a cohesive pattern around what I would say to this creature that would buy me enough time to figure out what was going on, but matters rapidly took on a life of their own. Seconds after I rang the doorbell, I heard high pitched screaming coming from inside the house. Without hesitation, I threw myself against the front door, but it held. Simultaneously, I yelled out. "Police! Open up!" I kicked the door solidly this time and it popped open, carrying me with it. I spilled into the foyer, falling to the floor. My head turned to the left and I could see down the hall. In front of me was the demon. He stood there in shock, some grocery articles in his hands. A split second later, his shock became anger and his demeanor changed as he tossed the items away and rushed toward me, pulling a huge knife from a sheath on his belt. But behind him, I could see the cause of all this commotion.

A young woman, naked, bruised, bloody, and dirty, stood a little further down the hall behind this man on the left side of the hall, screaming at the top of her lungs. It all happened so fast after that. I'm left handed. When I fell, I instinctively rolled so my right shoulder hit the floor. My gun hand was still free. The demon was almost on me when I raised my Bersa and fired three shots center mass into his chest. He stumbled back from the force of three 230-grain .45 caliber hollow points hitting his chest microseconds apart. He looked down at the blood flowing freely from his body, looked at me as though to say something, then fell to the floor, bleeding out in less than a minute.

It took me a second to pull myself together. My ears were ringing from the shots and I could hardly hear anything. I looked at the monster, then at her, and struggled to my feet, moving toward the girl. Her eyes were enormous, and she was trembling violently, although she had stopped screaming. I got within six feet of her and she drew back, stark fear in her eyes. I stopped, put the Bersa in my concealed carry holster, and then held my hands palms out to her, not drawing any closer. "Easy," I said, looking into her eyes. "It's over. He's dead and won't hurt you anymore."

For as long as I had been hunting child predators, this was the first time an actual victim was alive and had seen me kill another person. All the other times involved dead bodies or just the monster himself. Tonight was unique. From the look of things, I had just rescued a victim who was being tortured and raped. I wasn't quite sure what to do.

I knew we couldn't stay here. My ears were still ringing from the gun blasts, they had been so loud. A forty-five is not a noiseless gun. Neighbors undoubtedly heard the shots. We needed to get out of here. "You're going to be ok. But we need to leave right now," I said. " I can't get involved with the police. Do you understand? I can't be seen by the police."

Molly still stood there, naked and shaking. She looked at this man who had killed her tormentor, then looked at the man lying dead on the floor. After pausing a second, she got control of her shaking. She looked down at herself. Dirty, bloody, naked.

"I'm naked," she said. Molly picked up the clothes strewn on the floor and walked into the bedroom. She could tell the man behind her was a nice man. He averted his eyes while she dressed, allowing her some modicum of privacy. Once she was decently covered, she reached for her hairbrush, but he entered the room.

"We don't have time for that. Bring your brush and anything else you need and let's go. I'll take you someplace where you can clean yourself up." Molly nodded numbly, moving as if in a fog, picking up a few items, but leaving mostly everything. They moved out into the hall towards the front door. Molly stopped at the kitchen table. On the table was her purse. She grabbed it and it seemed to give her some focus. She turned and noticed that while she was dressing, the man picked up the brass from the bullets. It turned out he was wearing plastic gloves, so fingerprints weren't a problem. Standing up from picking up the brass, she could hear ligaments popping and snapping, and she decided he was older than she first thought. For whatever reason, she trusted this man. For all she knew, he was taking her from one terrible place to another, but she didn't believe so. He reminded her of her dad before he died. Kind, but forceful. Thoughtful. Compassionate. She could see it in his eyes. They moved across the threshold of the door and out into the night. Behind her, she could hear the man close the door, as if they were going to come back.

For the first time in many days, Molly smelled fresh air. It smelled of rain and fresh evergreen trees. The air was intoxicating, and she stumbled and almost fell, so overcome with the scent. He moved to catch her, but stopped short of actually touching her, which she appreciated. She'd had enough of a man's touch for a while, if not forever. An experience such as she had endured could be enough for a person to switch sexual identity.

"My truck is over this way." I gestured with my arm in the direction I wanted her to go. I was pretty nervous and getting more nervous each second because the girl wasn't moving fast enough to suit me and I felt exposed. But at least she was moving. I would have to learn about her story later. We reached the truck, and I opened the door for her. She climbed in, placing her purse in her hands on her lap. I shut the passenger door then and moved to the driver's side, climbing into the cab. I started the truck, and we pulled out of the driveway. It seemed a miracle no one in the neighborhood appeared to be interested in the goings on at the big house at the end of the street where we came from. I found out later from the news that the house was specially insulated to keep noises from escaping to the street. The neighbors never heard the gunshots over their televisions and family noises. How ironic. The monster had fixed his house so no one could hear him as he tortured and raped his victims. In the end, no one heard him being shot and dying on the floor of his own home.

Chapter 51

After some encouragement on my part, the girl told me her name was Molly. I thought the name suited her. It was remarkably unique, special. While we drove down the road toward my trailer, I kept looking in the side mirrors, expecting to see the blue lights of a police car in pursuit of us. Molly was exceptionally quiet, not saying too much. She shivered again, despite the heat being on and the outside temperature not being that cold. I reached behind me and pulled out a blanket I kept on the backseat of the truck. I helped get it wrapped around her, but left her pretty much alone with her thoughts. She looked awfully young and had survived a pretty intense ordeal that probably would have ended in her death. She deserved some downtime, and I gave it to her.

We reached the park and I pulled up in front of the trailer. Molly looked up from her thoughts and took in where she was. "We're at an RV park," I told her. "I have a trailer here. You can clean yourself up and I'll fix us something to eat." I turned the engine off and opened my door. Then I came around and opened her door so she could get out. Molly stepped down from the truck onto the asphalt where the trailer sat. I walked the few steps to the trailer door and unlocked it. Opening the door, I stepped up into the interior.

I deliberately left the door open and didn't try to pressure Molly into coming in. I wanted to build her trust. She stood at the base of the little step up for a minute, then came into the trailer. I motioned her to a seat at the dining table while I searched the cabinets for a fresh towel and maybe a change of clothes. I wasn't too sure about the clothes. After all, they were men's clothes and I'm a big guy. They would look ridiculous on her. But it would only be for one night, I assumed. I sat down at the dinette table across from her.

"Molly, I need you to listen to me. I didn't take you to the police because I can't get involved with them. I'm not a bad person for what I'm doing, but the police won't see it that way. Do you understand? You're welcome to stay here for a bit with me if you want. I won't hurt you. You are safe with me. Understand? You are safe with me. If you want to leave and go to the police on your own tomorrow, that's fine. But I can't be there."

I sounded like a broken record. I knew that. She needed to comprehend what I was saying. She weakly nodded her head. "Good," I said. "Here's a fresh towel, and the shower is right there," I said, pointing over my shoulder. "Soap is in the little tray on the shower wall. While you do that, I'll fix us something to eat."

Molly got up and moved to the bathroom, closing the door. I wished now I was at a full hookup site, but this should be fine. The holding tank for gray water on a Rockwood trailer is pretty big. Even if she used all the water, that was still fine. I could either shower in one of the RV shower stalls, or go without until we got home. Everything would work out. I forgot to ask what she wanted to eat, but before I could knock on the door, the water started so I figured I would fix a couple things and let her choose.

For me, hamburger and rice was always an easy favorite, so I put some water on to boil. In case Molly was a vegetarian, I pulled out what vegetables and fruits I had, along with a few slices of bread. I set all this on the dinette table as Molly emerged from the bathroom, a towel around her head and dressed in a spare pair of my pajamas. She looked adorable and reminded me of my daughter Rachel, now interning at a photography studio in Phoenix, Arizona. We were somewhat estranged and didn't talk too much. I loved her deeply, but she had drug issues.

Molly looked at the spread on the table and sat down.

"Thank you," was all she said.

"Go ahead, get started." I told her. "I'm making hamburger and rice as well. It will be ready in a few minutes." Molly nodded, not saying anything else. She reached for a piece of bread, buttered it with her knife, and ate deliberately, chewing methodically. I had to wonder what she had been living on and for how long for a simple slice of bread to taste so good.

The hamburger and rice finished cooking, so I put some in a large bowl for both of us and placed the bowl on a trivet, squeezing the bowl in between the vegetables and bread. I motioned to her plate, gesturing if she wanted some. She nodded, so I picked up her plate and dished up some of the hamburger and rice concoction on to it, then I spooned some for myself, along with my own slice of bread and butter.

"It's not fancy, but there's a lot of it, so eat your fill. Tomorrow we can go shopping and stock up on things." After I said that I remembered I was heading home and, with luck, would make it to my house late tomorrow afternoon. I decided to wait and discuss that topic with Molly tomorrow after breakfast.

We finished our meal in relative silence. I wanted to hear her story, but it would have to be when she was ready, and maybe she would never be ready. I was eager to know why she didn't kick up a fuss about not going to the police right away, but she was mum about that, and I let it be. She undoubtedly had her reasons.

While Molly finished her dinner, I set up the bed in the other room for her to sleep in. When she finished eating, Molly turned to look at what I was doing. When she saw the bed, I saw conflict in her eyes. "It's ok," I assured her. "This is for you." I pointed to the dinette table. "That makes into a bed as well. I'll be sleeping over there." While I explained this, I stopped smoothing the quilt for the bed, awkwardly waiting to see if there would be a problem with what I said. Molly sat, still turned toward the bedroom, taking things in. At last she turned back around to finish her meal, said "Ok." And that was that. I finished the bed, then cleaned up the meal, washing the dishes while Molly sat at the table, staring into space. After I finished cleaning up, I went into the bathroom to do my own business and brush my teeth. It had been a long night, and I was ready to call it a day. Molly was still at the table when I came out. I could see why. For her to get to the bedroom, she needed to pass uncomfortably close to me if I wasn't in the living room where the TV was. I moved there now and Molly stood up. Without another word, Molly went to the bedroom and pulled the privacy curtain across to the other side. A moment later she turned back an edge and looked around the curtain, directly at me, her eyes filled with gratitude and tears.

"You remind me of my father. I trust you. Thank you for rescuing me," was all she said. Molly then let the current fall back into place and everything was quiet after that.

I collapsed the dinette and made up my bed, happy that Molly felt safe. I wanted to check the news but was just too tired. Climbing between the blankets, I dropped off to sleep within minutes.

CHAPTER 52

Molly thrashed around a bit that night, and screamed once, but the scream was short. I was a little concerned someone might come to the trailer and make an inquiry, but no one came. I drifted in and out myself, sleeping fitfully. Killing someone in front of someone else can be traumatic, as you see in their eyes the reaction of someone being murdered. I pondered it for a while, wondering what Molly and I should do about the whole situation.

It was early afternoon before Molly pulled back the privacy screen and emerged to sit at the dinette. I awakened hours earlier and morphed the bed back into the dinette table, trying to be as quiet as possible. I could have left the trailer, I suppose, but it felt better sticking around in case Molly woke up and needed something.

"Good afternoon," I said cheerfully. I was sitting in my chair, watching TV, but swiveled around so I could talk to her. "How are you feeling today?" Molly contemplated her answer before replied.

"Okay, I guess. Tired, sore. It feels weird. I'm out of that situation now but it's hard to process it's over. I expect to see him and he drags me back to that room and-and-and-" Molly stopped there. A tear ran down her cheek. I wanted to rush and put my arms around her, but knew that wasn't the right thing to do. I leaned forward in my chair.

"Molly," I began. "You've been through a horrible experience, but now it's over. He'll never bother you again. Let me get you some coffee. You drink coffee?"

Molly nodded, so I went to the kitchen and poured her coffee from the pot I had going on the kitchen counter.

"Do you have any cream and sugar? I like it sweet." I reached into the cupboard above the stove and took down the sugar. Then I opened the refrigerator and put a creamer container on the table. "Thanks," Molly said, putting a couple spoons of sugar into the coffee and added some creamer. She stirred it and took her first sip in who knows how long. She settled back against the dinette seat, savoring the sweet taste of freshly ground coffee. "That's really good," she said. After pouring myself a cup, I returned to my tv chair, easing myself down onto the cushion. I liked that chair, plus it gave her some space. I took a sip of my own coffee, relishing the taste.

"You ready to talk about last night? I asked. Molly looked down at the table for a minute, then nodded.

"Yeah, I think I am.

"He never told me his name. He just came into my room and raped me. Sometimes, other things. But he never told me his name. He acted like he knew me, but I knew I'd never seen him before. I could never make him happy. Every time after he was done, he found fault with something and would hit me, or slap me, punish me in some way. After about a week or so, it became harder for him, you know.

He had trouble. That made him even madder. He would get so angry and scream at me, then hit me. He was always threatening to carve me up with that knife he always wore. I thought about trying to grab it, but was too afraid. He got more and more violent when he raped me. It really hurt. Eventually, I knew he would kill me, probably in that bed. I think he was going to kill me last night, but you showed up. I heard you ring the doorbell, and I knew it was my only chance, so I started screaming. And then you killed him." She stopped abruptly, as though she were a CD that suddenly reached the end of play.

I sat in my chair, rolling my coffee cup around in my hands. "He was an evil man, Molly. He deserved to die." I said quietly. She cocked her head and looked at me for a minute, then replied.

"Yes, he was. I'm glad he's dead."

Well, that was a relief. She wasn't some fool that thought all life was sacred. She seemed rather resolute about the whole thing. I rose from my chair, taking my coffee cup to the sink. I rinsed it, then placed it in the dish rack.

"Can I have some breakfast?" she asked. I smiled at that.

"Sure," I said. "I've got eggs, some bacon, cereal if you want it. I can make you toast. What'll you have?" I looked over at her.

"Do you have any peanut butter?" she asked with a shy smile.

"I sure do, but it's the creamy kind, not the crunchy kind. The crunchy kind hurts my teeth." Molly smiled fractionally.

"Creamy peanut butter is ok. I'd like some toast, please. And more coffee?" I reached for the pot and filled her cup. She fixed it again and got that dreamy look in her eyes. "That is so good," she said. "I could drink a gallon of it."

"Terrific," I said. "I'm glad you like it. After breakfast, I'd like to take you somewhere to get you some clothes." She looked up at that and I quickly interjected. "Don't worry about that. But unless you want to wear my spare pajamas the rest of your life, we need to get you clothes." Molly looked sheepish.

"Okay," she said. "Let's go. What is your name, anyway?" I thought for a second, then figured, what the hell.

"David. My name is David," I said.

"Well, David. Thank you again for saving my life," she said. I raised an eyebrow. "You're very welcome," I replied. "Now, let me make you that toast."

The toast and her coffee were all she wanted. And another shower. An hour later we were down the road heading to one of the big box chain stores. I parked and we went inside. Two hours later, we emerged with a couple pairs of jeans, some blouses, underthings, plus toiletries for her like a toothbrush and stuff. Plus coffee. And ice cream. Because of the side trip last night, all my ice cream melted and I dearly love my ice cream.

On the way back, a sudden spasm of pain hit me and I lurched over the steering wheel, groaning. I pulled over to the side of the road and shut off the truck. Molly sat next to me in the truck, wide eyed. "What's wrong? You're in pain! Tell me what's wrong. Let me help you!" Molly could see I was in agony. Tears started to trickle down her face.

"It's going to be ok, just give me a minute." I reached into my jacket pocket and pulled out my pain medication. A partially filled water bottle sat in the center console holder. I grabbed it and took two of my pills. It would take time for them to work, so I had no choice but to wait.

"Molly," I said through the pain. I stated the obvious. "Molly, I'm a sick man. I'm on my way to my home in McMinnville, Oregon. I'll be better soon. But I need to get home." Molly kept nodding at what I was said, eager for me to get better. Slowly but surely, I improved, and my strength returned to me. I started the truck, and we were back on the road heading for the trailer. By the time we got there, I felt better, and we made our way inside after I parked.

I fell exhausted into my chair while Molly got me another glass of water. I felt better, yes, but I was weak. Molly took it upon herself to bring in the stuff from the car and saved my ice cream, storing it in the freezer. And there we sat, either staring at each other or closing our eyes, shutting out the world.

"So, I'm assuming you've got something bad, like the big C?" Molly asked. I nodded my head and made a C with my left hand.

"Yup. Caught the big one. According to the doctor, I should already be dead. I went into remission and was feeling pretty good. But, I think my remission period might be over. That's why I want to get home." I dragged myself up into my chair so I wasn't slouching so badly. "Molly, I need to get home. I feel bad. You don't owe me anything, but I wish you would come home with me. It's not a big place, but it's nice. You can have your own room, stay as long as you like. But you hardly know me and you've been through a horrible ordeal. I understand if you're not comfortable with that invitation." I stood, walking to the refrigerator to refill my glass with distilled water. "These pain pills really knock me out. Can you help me convert the dinette?" Molly shook her head.

"You were very nice last night to let me use your bed, and I'm grateful.

But it's your bed, and it's obvious you need it more than I do. I'm smaller than you, so this dinette bed will do me just fine. You get in there and get some rest."

I wanted to argue, but it was a really nice bed, custom made for the trailer. I didn't argue and stepped into the bedroom, pulling the privacy curtain across like she had the night before. The pills were kicking in, so I quickly pulled my clothes off and got into my pajamas. I tumbled into the bed and was gone.

Chapter 53

I woke the next morning feeling better, but still weak. The TV was on in the living room, turned down low. I lay there listening to the broadcast. Something was said about a man shot and killed in his own home, but it didn't get much press. Something told me our dead man was not well liked in the neighborhood. I sat up and put my legs over the side of the bed. I made some noise, and Molly peered in around the corner of the screen.

"Hey," I said. "I could have been naked." Molly smiled.

"No, not you. I don't see you as the sleep naked type. Now it's my turn to ask how you're feeling?" I looked at her.

"Pretty good," I lied. "Except I feel like shit." Molly smiled again.

"I made coffee. Want some?"

"Sure, sounds wonderful," I said, pushing up off the side of the bed to a standing position.

"After you," I said. She pulled her head back and moved the five steps needed to reach the stove. I walked out of the bedroom towards my chair and sat down heavily. "Any news about our friend?" I asked. Molly brought me my cup and set it on the little stand next to the chair.

"Not much. Big mystery why no one heard three gunshots from a large caliber pistol. But the police learned that once inside, you can hardly hear anything coming through the walls. They're accepting it's possible no one heard anything." Molly stood above me, watching the TV. She turned to look down at me while I sipped my coffee. "If the offer is still open, I'd like to go home with you."

Those words I had been longing to hear made my gut clench. I hadn't realized how lonely I was until Molly spoke. Although I'd known her only a few hours, I felt very paternal

towards her, like she was another daughter I didn't know I had. I was happy to hear she was coming to share my home.

"Thanks, Molly. Thank you. No strings attached. You're free to leave whenever you want." At that, Molly smiled and took my hand, leaning down to hug me. *Wow,* I thought. *I wasn't expecting that.* "Have you eaten?" I asked. She nodded. "Well, let me eat something and drink some coffee and we'll hitch the truck up and be home before it gets dark."

CHAPTER 54

My desire to get home quickly threatened to engulf me, so I ate some cereal with my coffee and called it good. I washed my face, brushed my teeth, and stepped out of the trailer into a glorious day. It only took minutes to hitch up the truck, and soon we were on Highway 101 towards McMinnville.

The ride home was amazing. Molly opened up to me and we started talking like we were old friends. She told me about her father, how I reminded her of him, and how he died in a car crash. About her mom and Barry, and what he did to her. As she told that part of her life story, I could see the pain in her eyes. It was unfortunate. If her mother had met someone else, Molly's life could have been very different.

I told Molly about Grace and our love of the outdoors. How cancer had claimed her, like it was now claiming me. I didn't tell Molly about my mission. Not yet. I wasn't done yet; I hoped. Perhaps I would go into remission again, if I was lucky. The hours flew by and soon familiar landmarks popped up and I talked to Molly about landmarks I knew in the area. What little I knew about the city I imparted to her. It only seemed like moments and we were at my house.

"Hang on," I told her. "I need to back her in." I pulled a little past the house and put the truck in reverse, slightly turning the wheel. The trailer crept around and without a mishap or a do over, I backed the trailer onto the pad especially made for it, jockeying around just a bit to get it straight, then killed the engine. "We're home," I said. Opening the door, I popped out, dropping to the driveway. Molly did the same. I opened up a side storage bin on the trailer and pulled out a tire chock and rammed it tight up against the wheel. Confident now that the trailer wouldn't roll away from me, I undid the hitch, the light cables and the safety chain, releasing the truck from its task of towing the trailer behind it. At last, I was home. I stepped back inside of the trailer to grab my ice cream and we headed for the house through the garage I opened with a remote, first turning off the alarm system that guarded the house. The service I hired did an excellent job of maintaining the lawn and shrubs. I appreciated that, left to me, the place would quickly turn into a disaster. I unlocked the door from the garage into the house and we stepped inside.

The house was musty, so I opened some windows to get a cross breeze. I went to the thermostat on the wall and turned the heat up a bit since humans were now occupying the premises. Then I gave Molly a quick tour. The garage door opened into the kitchen, so we moved through there to the dining room, then the family/living room with a gas fireplace and requisite large screen TV. I showed her the bathroom she would use and the bedroom I promised her. I showed her the small third room that served as my office. Then I led her to the backyard, which was quite large and flat. A six-foot fence surrounded it, so the curious neighbors were kept somewhat at bay. A few trees dotted the backyard, and it all looked very comfortable and perfectly suburban. The neighbors had no idea what I really did some nights.

Chapter 55

Lieutenant Anderson's day began with a hot cup of coffee with cream and sugar, and a fast food biscuit bacon concoction from a local fast food place. Making his way through the office to his desk, he stopped here and there to speak to various officers about their activities, laughing with a few others, and reminding still others of deadlines fast approaching. Finally, he reached his office chair and dropped into it after taking a large draught from the coffee in his hand, punching the on button of his computer as he settled into his seat. He watched the machine boot up and rotated his chair in a short arc, taking in the rest of the office. Stromberg was heading his way. *Please God,* he said to himself. *I just want to finish my coffee before my day turns to shit.* He sighed as Stromberg sidled up to his desk, dropping into the chair in front of the desk with an air of cockiness. Anderson eyed him over the edge of his coffee cup and raised his eyebrows.

"What puts you in such a fine mood this morning, detective?" he inquired. Jack held a piece of paper in his hand. It appeared to be a computer read out slip of some kind.

"I've been working on our vigilante killer theory. I think we're on to something. When you're done with your coffee, I'd like to show you the board I've built."

Anderson gulped back the rest of his coffee and stood up. "Let's go," he said.

They navigated through the maze of desks and conference rooms to one particular room. The room contained a bulletin board, a table with chairs, and a bookshelf stocked with outdated books on police procedure. On the desk were a laptop, a projector, and a small box with pushpins. Anderson smiled at that. It amused him to see old and new technology and methods merge together like this. Jack was at the bulletin board.

"I pulled the records you suggested," he began. "All registered sex offenders in Oregon, Washington, California, and Idaho. I then extracted all those whose deaths were determined to be accidents. Car accidents, choking, heart attacks, that kind of stuff. But I kept them as a subset of my master set. Several of these deaths that are left are deliberate acts, either in prison because, as you know, jailbirds don't like child molesters, or by any other deliberate means. On this list is our friend, Johnny Fields.

He's the only one in our immediate area. But it brings to mind my theory. What if we have a serial vigilante child predator killer, making his hits all look like accidents so that he remains beneath the radar? If you allow a rather large radius to his activities, a group of about nine people show up, all of them repeat child predators, all of them dead, all appear to be accidents, except for Johnny. What's unique about Johnny from the others? Nothing, really. But what if our guy uncovered that Johnny was himself a serial killer, but of innocent young children? Could that make him blow his stack, and, in a knee jerk reaction, kill Johnny?"

"But why did he call it in?" asked Anderson. "Why expose himself like that?" That dumbfounded them both, and they stood, thinking their own thoughts. Finally, Anderson spoke. "I think it's got something to do with the kids, not with Johnny. Once he discovered the bodies, maybe he didn't want them in the ground, especially the way we found them. It was pretty disrespectful, don't you think? The bodies were just dumped in a hole like you'd bury a dead animal. He might want to get them out of the ground as soon as possible. Maybe our killer has a real soft spot in his heart for kids." Jack looked thoughtful.

"You might be right. But how do we exploit that information? What kind of database keeps track of people with soft hearts for kids?"

"I don't know. But if we could find it, we might get some insight into this guy. I've got to go see the Chief but keep on this. I'm feeling if we could just focus long enough, we could find the pieces that put this all together." Anderson turned and headed for the office of the chief of police. Jack went back to his desk and pulled up the information they had and restudied it.

Chapter 56

I went to the breaker box out in0 the garage and flipped the one marked for the water heater. I made sure the pilot lights were on for the heater and the furnace, then went back inside the house. Molly was opening and closing cupboards, taking stock of what was sitting on the shelf. Most of it consisting of canned goods. We brought in the sacks of items I purchased the night we met and replenished the cupboards, and some items went in the fridge. Milk, eggs, bacon, meat, vegetables, stuff like that. The bread was on the counter, waiting to be consumed.

The fresh air coming in from outside cleared the rooms, and it began to feel like a home again. I dampened a couple of paper towels under the faucet so they were a little wet. On the way home yesterday, I had called ahead and the water company came out and turned the water back on. With the wet towels I began wiping down the countertops, removing the dust that invariably collects when a building sits idle for a while. I could hear Molly in her bedroom unpacking her things and getting set up in the bathroom that would be hers. I had my own bathroom in the master bedroom. Things were starting to come together.

Since it was getting late in the afternoon, I opted to prepare a more elaborate meal compared to our previous night's dinner. I pulled out a couple of steaks, an onion, and a couple potatoes. "I'm assuming you're hungry after our drive?" I said loudly so she could hear me. As I set the frying pan on the burner, I heard her say yes. While it warmed up, I took down a small plate to chop the onions on and set that out on the counter next to the coffeemaker. The bakers I put on another small plate and placed them in the microwave, which was above the stove. Normally I would put them in the oven and bake them gradually, but tonight I wanted to eat sooner and the microwave would have them soft and ready to eat by the time the steaks were ready.

"Molly, do you like cooked onions?" I asked. She replied yes. I slapped the steaks into the pan and they sizzled immediately, so I turned on the range hood and, with a muted roar, the fans came to life. After seasoning the steaks, I peeled the dry, outer portions of the onion and then cut it in half. One half I placed in a resealable sandwich bag and put in the vegetable crisper in the refrigerator.

The other I sliced and made short, slender fingers of onion destined for the frying pan at the proper time. I then pulled a can of green beans from the lazy Susan pantry under the countertop and opened it with the electric can opener nearby that sat on the counter. I had graduated from using manual openers to an electric one a few years ago. Manual can openers I found worked for about six months, maybe a year. Then they would get so tight my arthritic hands couldn't turn the handle. I finally gave up and purchased the electric. Not the most environmentally responsible choice for these times, but screw it. I was old, I hurt. Enough said.

I called down the hall and asked Molly to come out and get ready to eat. At the store, I purchased some favorite soda Molly picked and several gallon jugs of fresh, distilled water for me. I showed Molly where plates, glasses and eating utensils were and we set the table together, using paper towels for napkins. The steaks were almost ready, so I turned on the microwave for the potatoes, tossed the onions into the frying pan, threw the green beans into a saucepan and placed the saucepan over another burner. Within minutes, everything came together and with a flourish, I placed the steaks, baked potatoes and green beans on the table and we sat down to eat.

Having someone to share a meal with was amazing. Throughout my career, I endeavored to locate a lunch companion as I relished their company, and it provided a delightful reprieve from the monotony of my tedious occupations. Molly and I were chattering like old friends now, revealing insights to friends and events, or bursting into laughter at something recalled. I discovered we had a lot in common, and my affection for her grew even stronger. She was truly an amazing person.

For dessert we shared my ice cream, large bowls of it. It was truly a wonderful meal and a terrific homecoming event. When we finished eating, it was almost midnight, and I was exhausted, as was Molly. We said our goodnights to each other and went to our respective rooms. After using the John, I put on my pajamas, brushed my teeth and crawled into bed, turning on the bedside lamp, intending to read my tablet for a few minutes. I perused my email, Facebook and MSN to get the latest news. After that, I laid the tablet down on the bed beside me and fell asleep.

CHAPTER 57

After dinner, because it was so late, Molly retreated to her bedroom and prepared for sleep. She luxuriated under the covers; they felt so nice after the rough fabric she endured in that monster's house. She was beginning to feel clean again. But there was a pain in her heart, and a hole in her soul. She knew she would never be the same. This man she was with seemed a very nice person. Why she trusted him, she couldn't say, but he gave her a warm, protected feeling. She turned on her side and sleep overtook her in moments. And the nightmares didn't come. She slept soundly.

Chapter 58

We spent the next few days getting the house back up and running. I pulled all my dirty laundry from the trailer and started running it through the washer and dryer. On the road, I normally stopped at laundromats when necessary. Now it felt good to throw my dirty clothes into my own washer and start the machine using my own soap from a big box. I liked to use the pods, plus they did a pretty decent job getting things clean. Doing the wash was kind of fun, but I didn't care much for folding, though.

And I abhorred ironing. When a particularly wrinkled garment needed ironing, I resorted to the old bachelor's trick of tossing a damp towel into the dryer, which removed the worst of the wrinkles. I used to use dryer sheets to remove static from the clothes, but now realized it didn't make much difference. Perhaps because of the new fabrics, I didn't know. I only had a few polo shirts to hang up or fold. I wore mostly T-shirts. Which were comfortable and easy to care for.

Molly had left her environment without warning, so she had hardly anything and virtually nothing I hadn't bought for her at the store. Her purse held a few items, but she was literally starting over and it was going to take some time to build up her wardrobe. She seemed ok with that and didn't appear worried. The two of them dusted everywhere, wiped surfaces down with damp towels where needed, and vacuumed the rest. By the end of the day, the house sparkled with new life.

One evening, days later, they watched the news while eating dinner. I felt like it was back to square one in that respect. Unsurprisingly, channels with limited commercial interruption had an even higher concentration of commercials. Molly suggested to me perhaps we could subscribe to Netflix or something to get some movies and I was okay with that, intending to sign up the next day. When I was traveling, I didn't watch much TV except at dinnertime, and that was usually the news. I liked movies, but really preferred to read. However, I didn't have a problem subscribing to a service. I should probably look into a satellite service as well, although dish services seemed overly expensive for what you got. But I wanted both of us to be happy.

Molly was watching the television when she realized David wasn't there anymore. He had excused himself to go to the bathroom, but had been gone for a pretty long time. With his history, she worried about him, so she got up from the TV and walked down the hall. She found him in the office bedroom, eyeing some database. A notepad lay to his left, and he held a pen in his left hand. It appeared he hadn't heard her come in. When she called his name, he jumped. "Sorry," she said. "I thought you heard me. What are you looking at?" He looked at her pensively, then seemed to make up his mind, nodding to himself slightly.

CHAPTER 59

"I haven't told you everything about me, which I'm sure you're aware. It doesn't really matter so much now, because I'm sick again and I don't know how much time I have." I pushed my chair away from the desk. "Let's go into the kitchen," I said. "I need something to drink."

We moved to the kitchen, where I grabbed some ice water and Molly pulled a soda from the fridge. We sat down at the kitchen table. Molly sat, patiently waiting, while I sorted out what I wanted to say. Finally, I began.

"There's a reason I rang the doorbell where you were being held. But let me start earlier than that. My wife Grace was a social worker for abused children. My work was in management for the high-tech industry, pretty boring stuff, actually. Grace would come home and tell me about her day and how she helped struggling families with rent problems, or finding a job for the parents, maybe help to get food stamps, things like that. It all sounded so much more important than what I was doing. I shared her enthusiasm about her work and what she could accomplish by helping people."

"What disturbed us, though, were the depraved things. Kids from broken homes. Children molested by their own family members. Children murdered and their bodies hidden to cover up the despicable things done to them by neighbors, family, and strangers. It left us cold. Grace sometimes came home crying over a particularly horrible situation she could not fix. It would break her up inside and I would hold her on the couch as she cried, comforting her until she felt better. On TV, we sometimes learned about child predators released, their cases dismissed due to a technicality, or a judge who imposed a sentence on a man that was hardly more than a hand slap. That person would fulfill his time quickly, especially with good behavior, and then would be out on the streets again to do what the evil in them compelled them to do. In my mind, I vowed if I ever came across someone molesting a child, I would not hesitate to put a bullet in their head and save the state the cost of a trial."

"When we retired, we bought the trailer and became state park volunteers, roaming the parks within three states, performing work that earned us a free camping space. We did this and loved it until Grace passed away. I kept on doing it because I enjoyed it, and it made me feel like Grace was near me. I miss her so much."

"Then I found out I had cancer. A very potent cancer. It's spreading quickly through my body and the prognosis isn't good. But I was sitting in my chair in the trailer over in Bandon, when a notice of a child molestation came on the news. I became curious about child predators, more so than I had before. I discovered there are databases where records are kept on sexual offenders. And some explicit to child sex offenders. I spent some time going through one of these databases, and I came across a Michael Bateman. He was a convicted child molester and was supposed to be registered. For whatever reason, I had my suspicions, and I decided to check him out. I discovered he worked at an elementary school and violated his parole. I called the police and told them this, thinking they would jump on it and apprehend him. They made no attempt to arrest him and remove him from that school. I was furious. I called them again, but they were more interested in finding out who I was than in taking what information I could offer on Bateman and arresting him."

"Then Bateman kidnapped a little boy. I think it finally came out the boy was dead, and they found him in a dumpster behind some store. Isn't that pathetic?" I asked. Molly nodded. "Something inside me snapped. When I saw the story on TV, I called the police yet again and yelled and screamed at them. After that, I decided to take matters into my own hands. As I move around the state parks, I make lists of convicted sex offenders, or offenders who got off on technicalities. I stake out where they live, where they work. If I can find evidence they are still abusing children, I exterminate them. They are little more than vermin. I've been doing it for over a year. I try to make it look like an accident so I can keep a low profile. In your case, I was in the store getting groceries and I sensed your monster in the checkout aisle next to me. I could feel his evil and instinctively knew something was very wrong. I followed him home. The rest, you know." I finally stopped. My throat was dry, and I was a little out of breath from talking so much. I watched for Molly's reaction. She sat there, taking it in, trying to process it. I couldn't help but wonder if I had done the right thing.

Finally, she spoke. "This murder you do," she said. "Do you enjoy it?" I glanced at the ceiling, then down at her.

"I don't enjoy it. But I get satisfaction from it. I'm removing evil from this world, one asshole at a time." Molly returned my gaze.

"You know they'll catch you eventually, right?" she said. I gave her a little smile. "Doesn't matter, really. It won't be long before I'm gone. Certainly, before any trial can be convened. If I spend the last few months of my life behind bars, so be it. I did my part to make this a better place." That last part sounded a little corny, but I let it go.

Molly contemplated this new knowledge about her friend. My veneer had a little stain on it, but it was certainly in a good cause. A noble cause, she thought. "When will you go out next?" she asked me. My gaze fell to the clock on the wall near the fireplace.

"I'm surprised and relieved you are taking this so well. I wasn't going to go out until you felt better and I knew more about you. That said, I could go out tomorrow night after I make a few preparations." I told her. Molly smiled.

"Awesome. I'd like to go with you."

Chapter 60

Stromberg's search for child sex offenders that were victims of sudden death through trauma or otherwise picked up a sudden death by gunshot in Crescent City, California, just south of the Oregon border. Although it wasn't in their jurisdiction, Anderson asked the California police if they could visit and talk with some of the officers and other personnel involved in the discovery.

Lieutenant Anderson received a reluctant yes and with the okay from the Chief they were in a police car traveling for the border within the hour. Anderson expected to stay overnight at least, so he called while in transit to reserve them a room at the Lakeview Guest house. It was the best room he could find. The others were horribly more expensive, plus it was only for a night or two. Anderson and Stromberg arrived late in the day, and introduced themselves to local law enforcement. An officer drove them to the house where the murder took place, explaining what went down on the way.

"This house is kinda weird," said the officer. Jack and Lieutenant Anderson kept silent, and the officer continued. "Once you get inside, it gets real muted. No echoes, nothing carries. You have to raise your voice to be heard in the next room. We found the victim, Alex Jackson, deceased at the scene. He had three forty-five caliber slugs in him, bled out in seconds. He has a criminal record of some note, but he's been behaving for a while. Registered sex offender. Then we found the bedroom." Anderson's ears picked up on that right away. "Bedroom?" he asked. "Yeah, it was really creepy. Handcuffs at the head of the bed, leg restraints at the bottom. Stains on the bed consistent with blood and other fluids. Medical examiner gathered samples of hair and skin where the skin chafed against the handcuffs. The room has been processed, so you don't need gloves. All the samples are back at the lab, but you said you wanted to see the murder scene first. Here it is." The car turned onto a suburban street. At the back of the street, a large, majestic house stood. As they approached, Anderson could feel the eeriness of the place stretching out to him, but he knew that was just bullshit nonsense. The car pulled into the driveway and they got out. "Officer, do you have a name?" Anderson asked. The officer answered while unlocking the door. "Albert Fineman, sir," replied the officer. "Well, thank you for the lift. You don't have to come in with us. We've worked murder scenes before. We'll just be a few minutes." Anderson and Stromberg walked into the house, immediately noticing the large stain on the hardwood floor, indicated by a chalk outline on the floor surrounding the bloodstain. The two officers spent a few minutes looking over the kitchen and family room, then moved down the hall to the open bedroom. Forensics had taken a lot from the room for evidence. The restraints, the sheets, any clothing. There wasn't much to see, but there was a strong odor in the room impossible to ignore. An odor of sweat, blood, mold, and something else. The two smelled it and backed out of the room. "Man," said Jack. "That's wicked! What is that?" Anderson shook his head. "It's the smell of approaching death. Whoever was in here was close to dying. Albert! Anybody take note of the smell?" Fineman shook his head. "Wasn't that strong, before. No one seems to know where it came from." Anderson checked his watch, then spoke, "Ok, I've seen enough. Let's get out of here."

All three of them made a beeline for the door and didn't stop until they were outside, breathing the outside air deeply into their lungs. "Well shit, sir," said Jack. "That was downright nasty. Whew! Glad I'm out of there." Officer Fineman locked the front door behind them.

"Me too, sir," he said. Anderson looked around at the neighborhood for a minute, then climbed into the car.

Back at the station, Anderson and Stromberg reviewed the police report. As far as who shot Alex Jackson, next to nothing was found. No brass, no fingerprints, no photographs or film from security cameras, nothing. This guy was a genuine ghost. Their trip appeared to be a bust, so they thanked the captain of the station and headed to their hotel room, stopping off to eat at a local restaurant. While waiting for their dinner, Jack expressed his frustration.

"Man, when are we going to get a break with this guy? I can't get a bead on his methodology. If he's responsible for some of the murders in the report, I can't find anything linking them together. What about you?"

Anderson was drinking from his water glass when Jack posed the question, so Jack had to wait until he was done and set the glass back on the table. "I'm wondering if our killer isn't that guy who contacted the station a year or so ago. You know, the guy who yelled at us because we didn't pick up Bateman? He was convinced the boy Bateman kidnapped would still be alive if we had moved faster. Technically, he's right. We should have moved faster. I'm at fault for that by not giving it a higher priority. I have to live with that. But, have you noticed that after the Bateman case, we haven't heard from him since? What if he's decided to take matters into his own hands? Help us out, so to speak." While Anderson was talking, their dinner order arrived. After spreading his baked potato out and smothering it with butter and sour cream, Anderson cut into the New York Strip steak he ordered before speaking again. "Hey, that's a pretty tasty steak." He stopped talking long enough to finish chewing and then swallowing the medium rare piece of meat. "If by any chance the man we want is that guy, then the only clues we have really are the calls made to the station, which are hardly clues at all because they weren't recorded. One of our biggest problems is we don't know which murders to assign to our ghost. Some of these deaths, marked as accidents or natural causes, may not have been accidental. How do we figure that out? There's got to be a key somewhere that ties this all together."

Jack ordered a shrimp scampi with a side of clam chowder, embracing the culture of the town. He inhaled the aroma of his meal and dug in at once. When his boss paused in his musings, Jack offered his own perspective on the case.

"I know what you mean. This is almost impossible to decipher. We have no common elements that link them all together. There's got to be something." He stopped speaking, his fork halfway to his mouth. "I think I have something," Jack said. Anderson looked up from his steak, his eyes imploring Jack to continue, which he did. "Johnny Fields was killed with a gun, and Alex Jackson was killed with a gun. The murders were sloppy, poorly thought out.

What if it's our guy, caught off guard and acting instinctively? He reacts to the children's bodies at Johnny's house and kills him still strapped to the chair. Alex is near the front door, on his back, knocked down by three forty-five caliber hits. Maybe he was rushing our killer, who shot him in self-defense, more or less. Did you notice the size of the knife in the report? And this too. The angle of the bullets penetrating Alex's body suggests whoever shot him was on the ground. Remember, the door was busted in. Maybe our guy fell in after the door gave way." Jack became silent, looking over at Anderson, a glimmer of hope shining in their eyes. Anderson stopped working on his meal while Jack was speaking and they both stared at each other. Maybe they had their break. Just maybe.

"Let's finish eating here and get back to the hotel room. I'll see if we can pull any other clues from these two incidents. Good work, Jack." Jack smiled at the lieutenant.

"Only work I know how to do, sir, is good work." Jack said. Anderson chuckled, but didn't say anything. The rest of the meal was consumed in virtual silence.

Back at the hotel, the two officers logged into their laptops and accessed their police database. It looked like they might have a break in the investigation.

Chapter 61

I wasn't quite sure how I felt about Molly joining me on my mission, but she seemed eager to go. After telling me she wanted to come along, I slowly said okay. She was seventeen and able to make up her own mind, I felt. I showed her how to manipulate a sex offender database to create lists of predators near us. In a lot of cases, they included a list of crimes in the search. I might have been able to glean more information if I had a paid subscription, but I was apprehensive of the police.

Could they find me if I was using a paid service to find my targets? I didn't want to research that question because maybe even the question itself was enough to direct their efforts in my direction. I knew that Military and Homeland Security monitored transmissions, using sophisticated algorithms to extract keywords and statements from the ether based on a word index. Words like bomb, or explosive, revenge, key terrorist leaders, could lead to their apprehension. Maybe the police could do the same. I had no idea. Even if they said they didn't, I wouldn't believe them. Better safe than sorry.

Tonight, we were just going on a stakeout, a visit to one particular bastard in the area. Michael Harry Swan was a genuine piece of work. A long history of child sexual abuse warped his record. He spent time in prison, surviving the other prisoners who would kill him by savagely attacking them when confronted, until the other inmates were so afraid of him they didn't dare touch him. His last jaunt in jail was brief. His lawyer got him out on a technicality. What a shit. Well, given time, we were going to fix that.

We parked in the shadows down the street from his house. Michael was home, a fancy Lexus in the driveway. This particular excursion differed from the others. Swan was married, and had two kids. Could you believe it? Did his wife know he had a record? *What kind of woman would stay with a man who was a convicted child molester, much less have kids with him? Did she assume her kids were safe because they were his kids? I sure wouldn't make that assumption.* I turned to face Molly.

"OK, Molly. We need to be extra quiet when we get to the house. From what I see, he has a Ring doorbell, so we'll definitely avoid that and check out the side and back of the house. Are you sure about this? I asked her. Her eyes sparkled with excitement. She was really getting into it.

"I'm sure," she said.

"OK, then. Let's go."

We crept out of the truck, closing the doors gently. I looked around but couldn't see anybody looking out their windows at us. Even if they did, they probably wouldn't see anything. It was night, and we were dressed in dark clothing. If someone tried to look out from the inside of a lighted house, the brilliance of the light prevented them from seeing anything. It more or less destroyed their night vision. Both Molly and I wore sneakers, so our footfalls were virtually silent. It didn't take long to reach the side of the house. Light spilled out from several rooms and we could clearly see into the rooms. Swan sat near us in an easy chair, reading a book. The wife and kids were nowhere to be seen, which kept me on my toes. We watched Swan for a few minutes, but he made little motion other than to turn the page of the book he was reading. Things seemed awfully bland.

I regretted coming out tonight on Molly's first run. I should have waited until the day and see if I could get into the house. With everybody at home like this, he was unlikely to try anything inappropriate. This night was a bust. I turned to tell Molly we were going home when a stabbing pain hit me in the chest. I couldn't help myself and groaned, hopefully not too loud. That didn't matter at all, because I became quite dizzy and fell against the house with a loud thud, then dropped to the grass. Molly turned toward me and knew instantly I was in trouble. "David!" Molly whispered urgently. "Come on, we've got to get out of here." I climbed slowly to my feet and stood shakily in front of Molly, and ambled forward. Suddenly, I heard the click of a lock and the scrap of a door being opened at the front of the house, followed by an announcement by the Ring doorbell that however activated was being recorded. Swan had heard me. He was coming.

"Go, Molly," I croaked. "Get out of here. I'll take care of Swan." I struggled to pull out my Bersa from the holster. Suddenly Swan appeared around the corner of the house and saw us, a nine-millimeter semi-automatic in his hand.

"What the hell?" he cried out, then shouted "Cindy! Call the police! We have a peeping Tom." Then Swan saw my gun, and he quickly drew his gun up and shot me near the diaphragm. Molly screamed as I dropped. In a split second she crossed to me and in a single motion retrieved my forty-five from its holster, aimed it at Swan and pulled the trigger. A loud roar erupted from the barrel and a forty-five caliber slug emerged from the barrel and struck Swan in the heart, killing him instantly. Swan dropped his gun and fell to the ground. Molly rushed over to me, helping me stand again.

"Come on, David, it's not that bad. Let's get to the truck." Molly put one arm under me and we sort of limp shuffled across the lawn toward the truck. Swan's wife came out as we reached the truck and saw her dead husband's body and began screaming, looking right at us. Molly placed me in the passenger side of the truck and fumbled with the keys I'd left on the dash. The truck fired up and we jumped away from the curb. Molly turned the truck around, but I could see Swan's wife looking at us as we sped away. This was bad. Very bad.

I made Molly slow down as we sped through town and she lowered her speed to the limit. That helped to not getting caught by the police, but I was bleeding profusely. It was clear I needed a hospital. Molly drove me toward the nearest one. As we drove, she spoke to me. "David, you're going to be okay, right? You're not going to die. I won't let you die." Tears started down her face. "I'm not going to let you die! We're going to do this thing you do together. I want to be your partner, so you can't die.

You just can't!" But I knew different. "Molly," I said. "Get a grip. I think we blew it. This isn't for you. You need to be something better. Drop me off at the hospital, give a false name. Don't give them your name, and try to avoid the cameras. Don't get caught up in this.

You're young, smart, a girl I would be proud to have as my daughter." I stopped talking then. We were at the emergency care entrance to the hospital. "Try to keep them from reading your license plate number. When I'm out of the truck, tell them you're going to go park and drive towards the emergency parking area. Once they take me inside, keep going and get to the house. Take anything you want from there and then go." Emergency people were coming out to the truck. "I love you, Molly. Now get out of here."

The passenger side door opened and the emergency crew gently lifted me out of the truck onto a gurney.

"You'll have to come inside, miss, for the paperwork," one of them said.

"Right," Molly replied. "I'll park the truck and come in." the technician seemed satisfied with that and they rolled me on the gurney into the hospital emergency room.

CHAPTER 62

Molly pulled away from the emergency entrance and drove toward David's house, keeping just under the speed limit. What was she going to do? Her friend was hurt. He might even die! What was she going to do? She wiped tears from her face as she sped toward the house. On the way, she got the glimmer of an idea. By the time she reached the house, it had grown into a plausible plan. Pulling up to the front door, she popped out and raced inside. David had told her where the weapons and ammo were kept. She grabbed all that. She grabbed the laptop, monitor, charger and printer as well, arranging the desk so it appeared David had never owned a laptop. He was just an old, retired person. She stashed everything in the trailer, securing everything so it couldn't bounce around and break. Then she packed everything David bought for her and stuffed it in a couple suitcases she stumbled across while packing. The suitcases went into the trailer as well. All traces of her were pretty much obliterated. That done, she backed the truck up to the trailer, securing the hitch, safety chain and travel lights like David had shown her. Once she completed the hook up, she climbed into the truck and gently pulled out of the driveway, and rolled down the street.

Molly drove around until she found a motel that allowed parking in the back. She took a room there and signed in, saying she was staying a few days. She had to use her real name for the registry, but it couldn't be helped. Once registered, she unlocked her room and stepped inside. Finally, she could relax and think about her next move. It was obvious she would need to sneak in to see David, check on how he was doing. She hit on an idea she could implement in the morning. But for tonight, she was exhausted and needed some rest.

The next morning Molly used the free Wi-Fi of the motel to access medical supplies and found where she could get nurse's scrubs. She went out, bought the clothes, had breakfast, keeping an ear out for any gossip related to last night's events, but heard nothing. Back in her motel room she did some things to her face and hair to make her look older than she was. Once that was done, she went to the truck and unhitched the trailer, then drove to the hospital. Dressed like a nurse, she hung around the smoking area until someone came out the side door.

The people who came through were too absorbed in their own affairs to notice her and it was easy to wait until the door almost closed before she grabbed it and was inside. One thing she hadn't thought to grab was an ID tag, which everyone seemed to have. Molly thought she knew where she could get one and made her way to the nurses' prep area. She waited until one nurse stepped into a shower and while her back was turned, Molly lifted that person's badge and fastened it to her chest. It didn't look too much like her, but the hair was about the same. If no one looked too closely, she should be ok. Next, she needed to find where David was. She assumed he was in intensive care. One thing she didn't know was whether or not he was under guard because of the bullet wound. All medical facilities are required to report these kinds of injuries, but some hospitals did it faster than others. With luck, she could get in to see David before he was arrested.

Molly found a directory and swiftly determined where the ICU was and headed in that direction. It was up a couple floors and towards the back. If she could figure a way to sneak in and out through the back stairwell, it would be easy to visit David and remain hidden. She rode the elevator to the third floor and headed toward the ICU. No police yet, which was a good thing. At the entrance to the ICU, a nurse sat at a station like a guardian protecting the ICU patients. Molly hesitated before approaching the desk. She kept out of sight so the head nurse wouldn't get suspicious. A couple of nurses drifted by her and when she focused, she could tell they were talking about a gunshot victim in room 357. That was all Molly needed. She waited until the head nurse left the station on some errand and edged past the station, looking for 357. It was about eight doors down, well beyond the station, and it turned out a stairwell door sat right across from it. How convenient. Molly pushed open the door and walked into the room and there was David, sleeping, apparently. She stood over him for a few moments, then turned to go, but he opened his eyes. "You're here." He said in a small voice. "I'm so glad." He murmured. "Come sit with me for a while, Molly. Please." Molly came around the end of the bed and sat next to him, taking his hand.

"Looks like you're still alive," Molly said. David got a strange look on his face. "What's wrong?" she asked, suspecting the answer.

"I'm dying, as we both know, just a lot faster than we thought," I told her. "The cancer has returned big time, and the gunshot tore me up pretty good. I've only got a few days, they said. The doctors might just keep me here until I'm gone, I don't know. I wouldn't mind. A couple of pretty nurses are here to brighten my day." I chuckled. "Don't think Grace would mind too much. I'll see her real soon. Have you thought about what you're going to do?"

Molly looked at me for a long time. "I'm going to do what you were doing. I want to kill every last child molesting bastard on the planet, like you were trying to do." Despite my objections, she shook her head. "You can't talk me out of it. My minds made up. I think it's something worthwhile to do. Anyway, I took everything out of the house that matters, plus I took the trailer. I need to figure how to get the truck and trailer in my name so I don't get picked up, but I can work that out. I've got your cards, so as long as you don't report them stolen, I'll be fine." We both chuckled at the implied humor. "I'm going to miss you. You're the father I lost in that car accident, and here I am, losing you again. It's not fair." They both sat in silence for the moment, then I said what I thought would be my last words to her.

"You should go. I don't want you to, but I don't want you caught either. You've made up your mind. I can respect that. Plus, you can stop whenever you feel you've done enough. Just so you know, there's a filing cabinet in the trailer that has the titles to the trailer and the truck. I keep important documents with me when I travel. That should help you get things sorted out. Now please, go. If I live, which I doubt, I'm sure I'll spend the rest of my life in prison. But that's ok. I'm tired, and Grace is waiting for me. Go on, get out of here."

I looked at her with the love a father has for a daughter, and I smiled. "Make a difference, Molly. Change the world. Kill every one of those god-forsaken bastards. Few will thank you for it. Few will understand you. But some will rejoice in what you're doing. Those who are suffering because of these bastards will praise you for what we are doing. Do the best you can. Try not to get caught. I love you with all my heart."

I sank back against my pillows, exhausted, but at peace. Molly stood, leaned over the bed and kissed my forehead.

"Goodbye daddy, I love you too," she said. She wiped a few tears from her eyes, picked up her purse, and left the room.

I felt very satisfied with the little I had accomplished. I had made a difference. I had saved lives. Others may call me a vigilante, but I call myself justice. I was happy to go with the legacy I had established.

Chapter 63

Lieutenant Anderson and Stromberg returned to the precinct with a couple of new ideas regarding their slippery quarry. While it was determined that a nine millimeter was used on Johnny, ballistics revealed the bullets came from Johnny's own gun. There was still a chance they were on to something and they dove into the evidence again, starting from scratch. Around one PM Mace stuck his head into the room. "Lieutenant, detective, there's a call for you from McMinnville police department about a shooting?" Anderson looked at Jack with a question in his eyes.

"Ok, Mace," said Anderson. "Put it through." Mace nodded, left the room and a few seconds later Lieutenant Anderson's phone rang.

"Hello, this is Lieutenant Anderson here. Who's this?"

"Sir," the person on the other end began. "I'm Sargent Brown of the McMinnville police? My Lieutenant asked me to call you guys. He heard about that case you've been working on." Sargent Brown paused. Anderson looked at Jack, wondering what this was all about.

"And?"

"Well, sir, there's been a shooting up here and a man is dead. The wife got a glimpse of the truck the alleged killer was driving. It was actually a late model truck, a big one, like an F150 or a Dodge Ram." Sargent Brown stopped again. It's like pulling hen's teeth on this guy, thought Anderson.

"What about this shooting, Sargent? How does it affect my case?"

"Well, sir. The medical examiner thinks the weapon used was a forty-five, and our database shows the man killed was a registered sex offender, served time. Does that mean anything to you, sir?"

Anderson was all ears now. "Sargent, I know this shooting isn't in my jurisdiction, but your lieutenant is right. I think there's a connection. Can you send me a copy of the incident report?"

"Uh, yes sir, we can do that. I'll do it right now," said the Sargent.

"Thanks, Sargent," Anderson told him. "You may have given us the breakthrough we've been looking for."

"Well, sir, glad to oblige, sir. I'll send that report right now." With a click, he was gone.

"I think we just got a break in the case. Sex offender in McMinnville was shot with a forty- five caliber weapon. Sounds like it might be our guy. Wait, the report just came up. I'll forward a copy to you." Shortly, Jack acknowledged receipt of the file. They both examined it and it turned out the murdered man's wife could remember the first two letters of the license number.

Anderson was exuberant. It wouldn't be long now they would have their man. Seven possibilities of suspects appeared on a license plate search. Shortly, they received a followup report that a gunshot victim had been admitted to the McMinnville hospital. Since it started out as their case, the McMinnville lieutenant invited Anderson and Jack to come help with the arrest. Although tired from their romp to California and back, Anderson and Jack quickly said yes and in a couple hours were in a helicopter heading for the McMinnville police station.

Once at the station, they ran the possible suspects and began to track them down. When they hit David's information, Anderson and Stromberg were certain they found their man.

EPILOGUE

Molly surfed the net, monitoring the news, blogs, and forums for anything related to child sexual predators. She kept shaking her head as the news was confirmed repeatedly. There were thousands of the bastards at large. And that was just the recorded ones. Her work would never be done.

She jotted down a few addresses and donned her coat. In the garage she checked the Bersa 45, a pistol grip 12-gauge shotgun, glasscutter, lock picks and other gear in her duffel bag. Starting the truck, she made sure her laptop was plugged into the recharge socket on the center console. Pulling out of her garage into the street, she headed north toward a destination a few miles away.

Tonight she would just observe, but if an opportunity presented itself, she would gladly punch the ticket of this bastard.

END

I hope you enjoyed reading *Vigilante Justice* as much as I enjoyed writing it. It's a painful subject, yet one I am passionate about.

If you'd like to learn more about me and my upcoming books, please visit *officialdjarvis.com*. You can also drop me a line, or a review, at *info@officialdjarvis.com*.

www.ingramcontent.com/pod-product-compliance
Lightning Source LLC
LaVergne TN
LVHW100921110826
845155LV00035B/40

* 9 7 9 8 2 1 8 9 4 3 8 8 2 *